THE BEAR TREE
and Other Stories
from Cazenovia's History

Erica Barnes and Jason Emerson

THE
BEAR
TREE

and Other Stories
from Cazenovia's History

Syracuse University Press

∞ The paper used in this publication meets the minimum requirements
of the American National Standard for Information Sciences—Permanence
of Paper for Printed Library Materials, ANSI Z39.48-1992.

For a listing of books published and distributed by Syracuse University Press,
visit https://press.syr.edu.

ISBN: 978-0-8156-3717-2 (hardcover)
978-0-8156-1132-5 (paperback)
978-0-8156-5542-8 (e-book)

Library of Congress Cataloging-in-Publication Data

Names: Barnes, Erica, author. | Emerson, Jason, 1975– author.
Title: The bear tree and other stories from Cazenovia's history /
Erica Barnes and Jason Emerson.
Description: First edition. | Syracuse, New York : Syracuse University Press, 2021. |
Includes bibliographical references. | Summary: ""The Bear Tree and Other Stories from
Cazenovia's History" examines and illuminates the unknown, unheralded, inaccurately told,
and long-forgotten stories of Cazenovia, New York"— Provided by publisher.
Identifiers: LCCN 2021002256 (print) | LCCN 2021002257 (ebook) |
ISBN 9780815637172 (hardcover) | ISBN 9780815611325 (paperback) |
ISBN 9780815655428 (ebook)
Subjects: LCSH: Cazenovia (N.Y.)—History—Anecdotes. | Cazenovia (N.Y.)—Biography.
Classification: LCC F129.C38 B37 2021 (print) | LCC F129.C38 (ebook) | DDC 974.7/64—dc23
LC record available at https://lccn.loc.gov/2021002256
LC ebook record available at https://lccn.loc.gov/2021002257

Manufactured in the United States of America

Contents

List of Illustrations   *vii*

Acknowledgments   *ix*

Introduction   *1*

The Bear Tree and Other Tales   *4*

The Sunken Canoe and the Legend
of the Indian Lovers   *9*

General Washington's Cook
*Former Slave and Revolutionary
War Soldier Settled in Cazenovia*   *17*

In the Shadow of Abolition
*The Unknown Lives of the Johnson Family,
Slaves to Cazenovia's Founding Father*   *24*

Jonathan Forman
*With Washington through
the Revolution and after*   *31*

1816
The Year without a Summer   *35*

First Grammar Book of the Ojibwe Language
Written and Published in Cazenovia   *40*

A History of Heartbreak
Who Was "Crazy Luce"?   *45*

The Mother of American Kindergarten
Susan Blow and Her Time in Cazenovia   60

William J. Hough Helped Create
the Smithsonian Institution   66

Elizabeth Smith Miller, the Original Bloomer   70

Escape from Confederate Prison
The Civil War Story of William Madge   75

The Men behind the Famous
Cazenovia GAR Photograph   81

Historic Connection to Abraham Lincoln
Francis D. Blakeslee, Cazenovia Resident and Seminary President   87

Lucia Zora Card, "The Bravest Woman in the World"   99

When President Cleveland Came to Cazenovia   109

The Cazenovia Mummy, Robert Hubbard,
and Generations of Interest   116

Theodore Roosevelt's 1900 Campaign
Whistle Stop in Cazenovia   123

A Family of Patriots
The Kent Brothers and Their World War I Service   127

"Nothing Further Remains but Our Duty"
Cecil Donovan's Letters from the Western Front   135

A Colorful Cazenovia Character
Circus Man Jim Fitch   146

The Ox-Bow Incident
*Great American Novel Written
by Cazenovia High School Teacher*   155

Bibliography   159

Illustrations

1. Samuel Forman   5

2. John Lincklaen   6

3. Cazenovia fishermen   10

4. Members of Cazenovia Lodge 900 of the
Independent Order of Odd Fellows   15

5. Plymouth Freeman's Revolutionary
War discharge papers   19

6. Plymouth Freeman's pension award   22

7. Attendees at the Anti-fugitive
Slave Law Convention, 1850   25

8. Lorenzo, the family home
of John Lincklaen   27

9. Drawing of Cazenovia Seminary
as it looked in 1832   42

10. Title page of John Summerfield's grammar
book of the Chippeway language   43

11. First page of "A Night of Years"   47

12. William G. Pomeroy Foundation historical
marker about Crazy Luce   57

13. Susan Blow   61

14. Froebel-style kindergarten room   64

15. Map of Cazenovia from 1852   67

16. Painting of William Hough and family   68

17. Bloomer costume   *71*

18. Elizabeth Smith Miller and Anne Fitzhugh Miller   *74*

19. The GAR Knowlton Post Number 160
Memorial Day photo circa 1900   *82*

20. Rev. Francis D. Blakeslee   *88*

21. Abraham Lincoln's signature   *92*

22. 1860 presidential campaign ribbon
supporting Abraham Lincoln   *93*

23. Lucia Zora Card with Trilby the elephant   *100*

24. President and Mrs. [Grover] Cleveland, c. 1893   *111*

25. Cazenovia mummy   *119*

26. Mummy undergoing MRI scan   *121*

27. Crowd at Lehigh Valley Railroad
Depot on William Street   *124*

28. Robert, Stanley, and Chester Kent   *128*

29. Jim Fitch performs acrobatic tricks   *147*

30. Jim Fitch performs acrobatic tricks   *147*

31. School yearbook photograph
of Walter Van Tilburg Clark   *156*

Acknowledgments

Writing a book takes the effort of not just the authors, but also numerous people who assist the authors along the way. We would like to thank the many people who gave us advice, assistance, and encouragement on the road to completing this work:

Betsy Kennedy, Elisha Davies, and the Cazenovia Public Library staff for their generosity and dedication to the cause of local historical preservation; Eagle News for allowing us to reprint photos and articles (in whole or part) from their archives; Madison County, New York, Historian Matthew Urtz; the Madison County, New York, Historical Society; Dr. John Robert Greene and the archives of Cazenovia College for their assistance locating Zora Card's educational records; Michael Roets, site manager, and Sharon Cooney, archivist, Lorenzo State Historic Site; Russ Grills, Cazenovia historian; Gene Gissin, photographer and owner of the historic Lehigh Valley Railroad Depot for sharing with us his photo of Theodore Roosevelt in Cazenovia; Chris and Judi Randall for allowing us to reprint their photo of Jim Fitch; Cazenovia residents Theckla Ledyard, Camilla (Davis) Viall, and William Dommett for sharing their reminiscences of Jim Fitch; Lynda Copper, antiquarian, without whom the world would not know about the GAR photograph and a nearly forgotten legacy of tolerance; Lincoln scholars Michael Burlingame and James Cornelius; Kim Nunnari and Lisa Phelps, descendants of Rev. Francis Blakeslee, for their assistance and permission to see and use the Blakeslee family autograph book; Lauren Leeman and the State Historical Society of Missouri; Lauren Sallwasser and the Missouri Historical Society; Erin Beasley, digital image rights and reproduction specialist, Smithsonian Institution, National Portrait Gallery, Washington, DC; Peter Huestis, Division of Imaging and Visual Services, National

Gallery of Art, Washington, DC; and the New York Almanack (formerly the New York History Blog) for previously printing our article on Plymouth Freeman.

THE BEAR TREE

and Other Stories

from Cazenovia's History

Introduction

Cazenovia is one of the jewels of Central New York, and yet few books have told its story—and those few were published long ago. Cazenovia's status as a beautiful lake town comes with a rich history of wealthy men who founded and sustained it. And most books and articles about this community focus on these wealthy elite and their grand mansions, the businesses they built and maintained, their churches, and the schools where their children were educated. Not much has been published about the everyday Cazenovia and all the interesting, outrageous, and fascinating aspects of this 225-year-old community.

This book is a collection of stories of the people, places, and events of this village throughout its history. But it is the unknown, unheralded, misunderstood, and long-forgotten stories that we present, such as the story of elephant and lion tamer Lucia Zora Card, "The Bravest Woman in the World," of world-traveled circus man Jim Fitch who performed acrobatic tricks on the Presbyterian church steeple, of the legend of the Indian lovers and their sunken canoe that still lies in the bottom of Cazenovia Lake, of the sad story of "Crazy Luce" who wandered the county for thirty years after her fiancé jilted her on her wedding day to elope with her sister.

Despite the relative obscurity of the stories we relate, many of the subjects involved had an effect well beyond Cazenovia, some of national and international significance. We examine tales that involve not just the greater Cazenovia area—Cazenovia village and town, the towns of Nelson and Fenner—but adjacent towns as well, including Chittenango, Pompey, DeWitt, and Syracuse. The people in the book lived, worked, served, or traveled in numerous places across the United States and around the globe. Cazenovia has connections to four US Presidents: Grover Cleveland and Theodore Roosevelt who visited Cazenovia, and local residents

1

who knew, met, and served in the military with the two greatest presidents—George Washington and Abraham Lincoln. Cazenovians also played major roles in national and world conflicts, including Revolutionary War Colonel Jonathan Forman, Civil War cavalryman William Madge (who escaped from Confederate prison), and heroes of World War I Cecil Donovan and the four Kent brothers.

The motivation behind this book is best summed up in the words of Henry Severance in his local history reminiscences of 1885: "To get out of the ruts of the travelled road and provoke discussion."

The few existing books concerning the history of Cazenovia tend to focus on the buildings, community fathers, and the so-called aristocrats of the area. The two best-known books of the genre are *Cazenovia: The Story of an Upland Community*, published in 1977 by the Cazenovia Preservation Foundation, and *Upland Idyll: Images of Cazenovia, New York, 1860–1900*, by Russell Grills, published by the State of New York Office of Parks, Recreation, and Historic Preservation in 1993. Both books give an excellent history of the founding of the community and its growth, and are filled with wonderful historic pictures, but give few insights into the interesting and personal stories of the average Cazenovian. The Cazenovia Preservation Foundation book, by its nature, focuses on the land, the buildings, and the architecture of the village, explaining their origins and uniqueness as a way to help preserve them for the future. *Upland Idyll* focuses mainly on the rich and powerful members of Cazenovia—who they were, where they lived, and their contributions to the community. Neither book explores the lifestyle of the common residents of the village, who they were, what they experienced, or how they lived.

The other two main history books about Cazenovia—*Owahgena: Being a History of the Town and Village of Cazenovia* by Henry Severance (1984) and *Cazenovia Past and Present (Madison County, New York): A Descriptive and Historical Record of the Village* by Christine O. Atwell (1928)—also focus on the town's founding, and then mainly describe the community through its sections, such as churches, schools, roads and railways, businesses, etc. Both of these books offer excellent factual information into the founding and the early years of Cazenovia, but give no personality to the community—no human interest stories, no interesting anecdotes, no reason to read them other than for piecemeal historical research.

Each story in *The Bear Tree and Other Stories from Cazenovia's History* represents the culling of resources from local, regional, and national archives and collections. Some records, like those pertaining to African Americans (both slave and free), were practically nonexistent and have been difficult to find and examine. Other records, like those of autograph collector Francis Blakeslee, were waiting to be discovered among forgotten family collections. With each story, a life that touched many others in its day is reexamined and celebrated. Our hope is that readers will come away with a renewed appreciation for the Cazenovia community that incubated and supported these artists, innovators, soldiers, and legends.

The Bear Tree and Other Tales

From Annals of Cazenovia:
1793–1837 by Samuel S. Forman

Samuel S. Forman was one of the founders of Cazenovia, having ventured
into the Upstate New York wilderness with the young Dutch land agent
John Lincklaen in 1793 to set up a community, assist in land sales, and
operate the store for the Holland Land Company. In 1837, at the request
of Mrs. Jonathan D. Ledyard, Forman wrote his "Annals" of the first settlement of Cazenovia. According to Cazenovia historian Russell Grills,
Forman's memoir "remains a most important document of the early settlement of Central New York." While many sections of Forman's "Annals"
are interesting to read, the authors have chosen to reprint "The Bear Tree
and Other Tales" because of its unique, bizarre (nowadays many people
may even consider it grotesque), and fascinating nature.

The Bear Tree and Other Tales

When the settlement [of Cazenovia] commenced bears were very plenty.
In the northern towns small game such as foxes, raccoons, minks, martins,
and weasels were abundant, a few otters were found in the streams, and
there were marks of beavers but none were ever taken. The lake abounded
with Yellow Perch (whence its name)[1] and with trout, suckers and bull-
heads or catfish.

---

1. Cazenovia Lake was known to the Haudenosaunee as "Owahgena," the Lake of the
Yellow Perch.

1. Samuel Forman in his later years. Printed with permission given by Cazenovia Public Library.

One winter a Mr. Walthers [Frederick Walters], a respectable German in the company's service, and myself were on the west side of the lake examining a lot of land which we had made a purchase of (the same which was afterwards called "the Cazenove lot") when as we were walking along our dogs gave the alarm that game was at hand. We hurried forwards and found them barking around a very large hollow tree, having encouraged them to attack, a small terrier dog on putting his nose to

2. John Lincklaen, portrait by Charles B. J. Févret de Saint-Mémin, 1796–97. Courtesy of the National Gallery of Art, Washington, DC.

a small hole at the roots was seized hold of and drawn almost entirely within the body of the tree. In order to rescue him we poked our sticks, when the animal within let go the dog, which ran bleeding home, and seizing the sticks held so fast that we pulled his nose out of the tree, but what creature it was we could not yet ascertain. We got a large pole and stuck the butt end into the hole and Mr. Walthers held fast the other end (as it were to a lever) while I ran to the farm house to get a gun and some hands with axes to engage in the combat.

On my return with the reinforcement, we found Mr. W. as I had left him grasping the lever and very anxious to be relieved from his state of incertitude. Our first business was to secure the hole where the stick was, which we did by driving into the earth large stakes, which we interlocked with logs. We then cut three windows in the body of the tree about four feet from the ground, making them about seven or eight inches large, so that we could have a fair view of the animal, which we then discovered to be, what we expected, a large bear. Having fired upon and wounded it, it became raving mad, raised its paws and put out its nose, gnashing its teeth fearfully and frothing at the mouth, its red eyes bespeaking dreadful retaliation were it at liberty. The gun was again loaded and fired, but again only produced a wound. As we were in perfect security, we paused awhile to observe how terrible his angry looks and actions were. A third time the gun was loaded and the shot proved fatal to poor Bruin, who fell lifeless.

We now cut one of the windows large enough to get him out and one of the men, after being satisfied that life was entirely extinct, went into the winter quarters of Mr. Bruin and after some heavy lifting our game was landed outside of its stronghold. The men got a hand sleigh, and placing the body on it, drew it on the ice over the lake to the village. It was dressed and weighed upward of four hundred pounds. It was a female and had two cubs in her. The skin was very black and finely covered. I gave the meat to the men, and four dollars for the skin, which afforded them much feasting and pleasure.

Another time when the jobbers had set fire to their clearing by the swamp, near where Mr. Lincklaen built his last house, the fire drove a large bear out and he passed through the village, no one being prepared to follow him he got off.

On another occasion a man passed a large one and her cub about a mile and a half up the Lake Road. He came to the store and informed us, whereupon we mustered about a dozen men and went in pursuit. We found them up a large leaning oak tree and commenced the attack. We had but one gun and no balls and were obliged to use therefore small slugs and shot. Having fired at the old one several times and perhaps hurt her, she all at once descended to a crotch in the tree, about twelve or fifteen feet from the ground, put her head between her fore legs, and threw herself off. As soon as she touched the ground, as many men as could stand fell upon her with clubs and other weapons, so that she never rose to her feet again. The next business was to get little Bruin who had ascended as high as the limbs would bear him. It was a little creature about half as large as a middling sized dog, and every time it was fired at would swipe with its paws; at last a shot proved fatal and brought it to the ground.

In the Town of Nelson not far from where the village now is, a terrible encounter took place between a bear and two men by the name of Bumpus of the Vermont Company. They saw a bear, fired upon and it is supposed wounded it, upon which it turned and coming up to one of the men seized him in a close hug. It happened that they were in the bed of the Chittenango Creek, which was shallow and has a strong bottom and the only way the man could save himself was by cramming the bear's mouth with stones, which his brother picked up and gave to him, thus preventing her from biting. They tussell'd in this manner until by some means they separated. The man was somewhat hurt but it did not injure him for any length of time. It was thought the bear had young near the spot which caused it to attack. It was a long time since Mr. Bumpus related the story to me.

At a place called Tog Wattles Hill, in Nelson about five miles east of Cazenovia, as a woman was washing near the house, her husband being off at work, a bear came up close to her and reared upon its hind feet, whereupon she caught up her child which was sitting a little way off and ran into the house.

They have been known to come in the night and try to get into hog pens, adjoining the log dwellings, when the noise would alarm the family, who would sally out and make war upon them. Down on the Gore they were very troublesome as were, also, wolves. These would come near the settlement and howl, but I never heard particularly of any damage done by them. A few deer have been killed near the lake.

These incidents may appear insignificant now, but at the time they created much interest and show that the settlement of a wilderness is attended with difficulties and dangers of various kinds.

The Sunken Canoe and the Legend
of the Indian Lovers

Sometimes, a modest discovery can have massive consequences for posterity. In Cazenovia, the finding of a centuries-old Native American canoe on the lake bottom more than 150 years ago was the catalyst for a legend that has captivated the community ever since—a legend of star-crossed lovers, tribal warfare, and tragic events.

On September 20, 1860, local fishermen John Fairchild, Ebenezer Knowlton, and Richard Parsons were enjoying some angling in Beckwith Bay on Cazenovia Lake when they noticed something unusual in the water. They pulled it to the surface and found it to be an ancient, rough-hewn dugout canoe filled with stones. The trio towed their find to the public pier and hauled it out of the water. It measured some twenty feet in length and was, according to one report, carved from a great red cedar tree and "had evidently been sunk intentionally by the Indians years before." The fascinating relic of a bygone era sparked great interest and curiosity throughout the village of Cazenovia, with people flocking to the pier to see the dugout and speculate on where it had come from and why it was there. The canoe became such a popular item of interest that the fishermen left it on the pier, where it became an unofficial village exhibit for all to see. "Its antique appearance excited much interest among the Cazenovians, and thereupon was kindled a flame of enthusiasm for the departed nobility of the race once the unquestionable lords of Lake Owahgena," according to historian Luna M. Hammond Whitney a decade later.

Word of the "Indian canoe" in Cazenovia eventually spread throughout the region. At some point, elders of the Onondaga Nation heard about it and told Cazenovia village officials that the removal of the canoe from

3. Cazenovia fishermen John Fairchild, Ebenezer Knowlton, and Richard Parsons pose with the rough-hewn dugout canoe they found on the lake bottom in Beckwith Bay in 1860. This photo was taken at the Cazenovia Lake public pier in 1861. Printed with permission given by Cazenovia Public Library.

its resting place in the lake was offensive and sacrilegious, and they demanded that it be returned to the waters of Lake Owahgena. The villagers thought it best not to anger their aboriginal neighbors, and so agreed to resink the canoe back into the lake—but not without a fitting and proper "Indian" ceremony first.

Why were the Onondagas so upset about the raising and removal of the canoe from the lake, and what was the canoe's story? Speculation was rampant at the time, and multiple stories were told about the canoe's origins. An inspector of the canoe when it was found declared that "it looked ancient enough to have belonged to the very first Indian who ever paddled." There were found "two or three wrought nails and scraps of iron" in the vessel, but that did not determine whether white settlers or natives made it, as those metal objects could have been obtained by the Indians through trade with Jesuit settlements in Onondaga in 1650 or 1670. So, according to reports in 1861, "its antiquity was considered to be satisfactorily established and all agreed to believe it."

But how, exactly, did the canoe end up in the lake, clearly purposefully sunk by being filled with rocks? One early historian declared simply it had been sunk by one of the local tribes as they left the area under attack from one of their neighbors "that the invading foe might not possess [it]." That story, fleshed out a little more through the years, was that the Oneida tribe, who considered the lake their reserve hunting and fishing ground, was holding a wedding ceremony on the shores of the lake when a hostile tribe of Onondagas attacked. Unprepared for the battle, the Oneidas, "gaily decked out in paint and feathers and religiously engaged in dancing and shouting to the beats of the tom-tom," jumped in their dugout (how an entire tribe fit in one twenty-foot dugout is not explained), crossed the lake and, upon reaching what is now called Beckwith's Bay, filled the canoe with stones, sank it, and fled through the forest on foot.

The most popular tale of the canoe, and what has become the predominant story, was first described in popular print in 1916 as the "Legend of Owahgena Lake."[1] According to this legend, Lake Owahgena divided the territories of the Oneida and Onondaga tribes, with the Oneida camp north of where the village of Cazenovia now stands and the Onondaga camp northwest of there, where the village of Oran now stands. Under the rule of the Five Nation Confederation, both tribes had equal fishing rights to the lake. This truce lasted for many years and, although the two tribes were not at war, they were also not on the friendliest of terms. One spring morning, a party of Onondaga returned to their camp with the news that the Oneidas had violated the treaty and were fishing on Onondaga territory. The Onondagas sent an envoy to discuss the situation.

The envoy, a young brave named Nakota, son of Chief Nagua, spent more than a week at the Oneida camp undertaking negotiations. During that time, Nakota fell in love with Princess Malaka, daughter of the Oneida chief, and "poured into her ears pledges of love, and wonderous tales of the lake country to the west." On the day Nakota was to return

---

1. The story was originally printed in the *Cazenovian*, the newspaper of the Cazenovia Seminary, "some years" before its 1916 appearance in the *Cazenovia Republican* newspaper, but that original publication has proven impossible to find.

to his camp, he told Chief Tewansah he loved his daughter and wanted to take her home with him, to which the chief replied that "as long as the moon journeyed across the heavens his daughter would never dwell in the land which lay across the Lake of the Yellow Fish." Nakota returned home empty-handed but, throughout that summer, would return to the shores of the Oneida camp at night where he and Malaka would steal away for a few hours. The Onondaga prince many times asked the princess to marry him, but she refused to oppose the will of her father.

Finally, Nakota decided the only way to win his bride was to force her into his canoe and steal away across the lake. According to the legend, Nakota and a band of Onondaga warriors crossed the lake one night intent on taking the princess. When they landed, they cut the thongs that held the Oneidas' birchbark canoes to shore, grabbed the princess and fled across the lake. Somehow, the Oneidas discovered the plan—either by the screams of Malaka or by an alarm raised by another tribe member who happened to be down by the water; stories differ—and the chief and his warriors gave chase. They ran to the lake shore to find their canoes gone and the kidnappers rowing rapidly away. The chief found a canoe higher up the bank that the Onondagas had missed, grabbed it, and gave chase with a handful of his warriors. His birch canoe was lighter and faster than the Onondagas' heavy dugout canoe, and the chief was soon upon them. Nakota then shot an arrow into the hull of the Oneida canoe, just below the water line, that caused it to sink. By the time the Oneidas got their chief to shore, Nakota and his band were safely across the lake and escaped.

A few days later, the wedding of Nakota and Malaka was celebrated in the Onondaga camp, and the newlywed couple took a wedding trip to the lakes of the west. Chief Tewansah, heartbroken and possibly hypothermic from his plunge into the lake, became ill and died a few weeks later. His final request was that his body be sunk in the lake at the place he had last seen his daughter, so his kin put his body in a canoe, towed it to the spot (the "shelf of rocks opposite the Shadow of the Pines"), filled the canoe with rocks, and watched it sink into the blue water.

According to Oneida Nation tradition, the story is slightly different. The Onondagas and Oneidas were feuding in the 1770s because the tribes of the Iroquois Nation had declared themselves neutral in the war between Great Britain and its colonies, but the Oneidas decided to side with the Americans. According to legend, a man from a prominent Oneida family and a woman from a prominent Onondaga family were married during the time of the tensions. Since the Onondaga Nation had felt betrayed by the Oneida Nation, the marriage caused great controversy and many people were angry about their relationship. The couple had to flee into Cazenovia Lake in a wooden canoe, but the canoe capsized and the couple died. The canoe was left in the lake.

Either way, the Native Americans in the Cazenovia area considered the removal of the canoe from the lake in 1860 an affront, and the villagers agreed to return it to the depths—after a proper ceremony. At 1 p.m. on Saturday, October 12, 1861, the "celebration" began with crowds and boats gathered around the canoe on the public pier. The boats were decorated with flags, while the participants in the "carnival" were dressed as Indians and had given themselves Indian names. Some of the prominent men and women at the event included "Medo-Howo" (Charles Stebbins Jr.), "Iagoo" (Ledyard Lincklaen, who was also the storyteller of the Legend of the Canoe at the event), and "Shaw-Shaw" (Helen K. Lincklaen), who portrayed the bride. At 2 p.m., the Indian warriors appeared, led by war chief "Natongura" (John Fairchild), and the event began.

The large group of people crossed the lake in multiple boats to Beckwith's Bay—including thirteen-year-old Jerome Lawson, who paddled the Indian canoe (and had to keep bailing out the water leaking in to prevent its sinking prematurely)—where a ceremony was held. According to news reports, the "council fire" was lighted, a dance occurred, and a short speech was made by Medo-Howo (at that time Stebbins was clerk of the village of Cazenovia and a few years later would become village president). He discussed the "sacred duty" they all were performing in sending the canoe back to its final resting place, and the hope that in the act "we may hope to escape those dire calamities which were denounced against those who should long disturb its rest. We may now hope that our corn may ever ripen beneath the autumnal sun—that our potatoes may not suffer from the blight and that, as in the happy event we celebrate, the course of true love may never be disturbed by the warring of hostile tribes." The assembly then adjourned and took the canoe to the shores under Eagle Pines to resink it in about eight feet of water. This ceremony was done by "Kokonoki" (Ebenezer Knowlton), one of the discoverers of the vessel the previous year.

This was not the end of the story of the "old Indian canoe" of Cazenovia Lake, however.[2]

In 1913, fifty-two years after the resinking ceremony at Beckwith Bay, the members of Cazenovia Lodge 900 of the Independent Order of Odd Fellows secured permission from the local Iroquois Confederation tribes to raise the canoe once again. This time, the intent was to place the canoe on display in the Cazenovia Opera House (today's Catherine Cummings Theatre on Lincklaen Street) to help promote the first-ever Odd Fellows fair held in Cazenovia. The fair was held for three days in mid-February, during which visitors could not only see the famous canoe but also purchase a small photo of it as a souvenir. When the fair ended, the canoe was returned to its watery grave in Cazenovia Lake.

Over the next five decades, the legend of the Indian lovers and the sunken canoe was an often-told tale in Cazenovia and in the pages of the community newspaper. Then, in September 1969, an expedition occurred on Cazenovia Lake to find and document the famous relic. Expedition leader Frank Bogardus said he had heard the story numerous times from several reliable sources, and he wanted to photograph the canoe "in the event it somehow should become lost or destroyed." Bogardus, who also happened to be the editor of the local *Cazenovia Republican* newspaper, published a page one, multipage spread of the story of his expedition, complete with underwater photographs of the canoe. Bogardus declared that the story of the canoe was tied to a local Indian romance that ended tragically, whereupon he recounted the story of Nakota and Malaka and their elopement flight across the lake. He said the sunken canoe is generally accepted, though unproven, to be the burial canoe of Chief Tewansah of the Oneida people. "Finding the canoe was rather anticlimactic,"

---

2. Just four years later, in October 1865, the *Cazenovia Republican* reported the discovery of "another canoe in Lake Owahgena" by local fisherman Richard Parsons. This canoe was longer and narrower than the 1860 canoe and was found in a different spot in the lake. Parsons tried to pull the canoe up from the bottom using an anchor, but it was stuck so firmly in the mud that he could not move it.

4. Members of Cazenovia Lodge 900 of the Independent Order of Odd Fellows posing with the dugout canoe in 1913. This is the same canoe found in the lake in 1860, which the IOOF obtained permission from the local Iroquois Confederation tribes to raise once again. The canoe was placed on display in the Cazenovia Opera House (today's Catherine Cummings Theatre on Lincklaen Street) to help promote the first-ever Odd Fellows fair held in Cazenovia. Printed with permission given by Cazenovia Public Library.

Bogardus wrote. "It was only about thirty feet offshore from the Stanley property, and in seven-to-eight feet of water. . . . Anyway, the purpose of our little expedition was to photograph the legendary relic in the environment where it had reposed for so long."

In more recent times, the story of the canoe's origins has been examined with more science and less romance. Some have argued in the pages of the *Cazenovia Republican* newspaper and elsewhere that the most likely explanation was that the Native American vessel was simply a fishing canoe that was filled with stones and purposefully sunk to protect it from the elements over the winter, as was typical practice long ago. Recent scholars believe the canoe actually had no connection to the area Native Americans, but was a remnant of the early white settlers in the area who would fish the lake.

Regardless of what American historians say about the canoe and its legend, members of the Oneida and Onondaga tribes believe the truth lies in the story of the star-crossed lovers from warring tribes who sought freedom for their love by fleeing across Lake Owahgena in a canoe in the late 18th century but died in the attempt. In 2015, members of the two tribes held two special ceremonies on the shores of Cazenovia Lake to celebrate reconciliation and help put the spirits of their ancestors at peace. The ceremonies came about because of the marriage of Neal Powless, son of the eldest living Onondaga chief, and Michelle Schenandoah, daughter of an Oneida Faithkeeper and granddaughter of a clan mother.

Schenandoah and Powless learned about the legend of the Indian lovers while they were researching wedding locations. When they realized the historic connection between their families and tribes and the legend, they knew their marriage was "destiny," as they said in a 2015 interview. So they held a traditional Native American wedding ceremony in the Onondaga longhouse where they first met and, the next day, had a traditional American wedding at the Brewster Inn on the shores of Cazenovia Lake. Before either ceremony, however, the couple participated in a healing ceremony on the shore of the lake. Members of the two families, dressed in full ceremonial regalia, gave an offering of tobacco to the water for the couple that lost their lives centuries ago to create a healing for their two nations and all Haudenosaunee people.

After more than 150 years as part of Cazenovia's lore, the Oneida canoe rests once more at the bottom of the "Lake of the Yellow Perch." As a bit of romantic speculation, it has captured local imaginations as few other stories have. The truth, however, remains shrouded in time and a thick aura of wishful thinking. Whether the canoe took part in the wild goings-on of runaway princesses or tragic brides, or if it was merely a victim of practical vessel maintenance left to molder, is something we may never know—and perhaps is an instance where the "truth" does not ever need to be known.

General Washington's Cook

Former Slave and Revolutionary War Soldier Settled in Cazenovia

In his 1891 memoir, Reverend W. W. Crane recalled growing up in the town of Nelson, on a farm three miles east of the village of Cazenovia. He attended school at Jackson's Corners, a half mile east, where he "fell in" with an African American boy he called "black Jerry." Crane remembered Jerry "though very meek and innocent, was so taunted, on account of his color, that he went to the brook and tried to wash off the black, and while his tears fell like rain drops on the water, he pushed his hand to the bottom and brought the sand and tried to scour off the black." The two became intimate friends, and Crane learned that Jerry's father had been a soldier in the Revolutionary War and General George Washington's cook. According to Crane, Jerry's father, Plymouth Freeman, an African slave before the war, also received his name from General Washington as well as his official Army discharge "in Washington's handwriting, which secured him a pension for life." A later newspaper article also reported that Plymouth Freeman "claimed to have been George Washington's waiter."

How is it that an African slave came to live in Cazenovia and, if he was actually a personal servant to George Washington, why is his story not better known?

Freeman was born in 1742. He claimed he was the son of a king in Guinea, Africa, and was kidnapped by slave traders as a child and brought to America. Nothing else is known of Freeman's early years until, at age thirty-five, he enlisted in a Connecticut regiment in the Continental Army in 1777 to fight in the Revolution. While Blacks were not allowed to join

17

the Continental Army early in the war, the policy changed in 1777 due both to the need for more bodies in the service and to the fact that the British had begun enlisting Blacks and offering them their freedom from slavery if they served the King. The Continental Congress, with the support of General Washington, decided to make the same offer to slaves, and it is estimated that by the end of the war, anywhere from five thousand to eight thousand African Americans served the colonial cause during the Revolution. It is unclear where in Connecticut Freeman lived, or if he was a slave or a free man at the time, but one state list of soldiers shows a man listed as "Negro, Plymouth" who joined in the town of Windsor, served 1777–82, and was listed as "not returned from the Army."

Freeman enlisted in the Connecticut line of the Continental Army in May 1777 to serve for the duration of the war. He served as a private in the second company, third regiment, and was paid $6.60 per month. All enlistees at the time were promised one hundred acres of land at the conclusion of their service.

It is difficult to ascertain exactly where Freeman was during the war and in what battles his regiment participated, due to the constant transferring among and between companies, regiments, and brigades, but the regiment's highest profile actions were in the final months of the New York and New Jersey Campaign of 1776–77. Freeman's regiment was one of the few in the Connecticut Line that was not at Valley Forge during the infamous winter of 1777. While Blacks serving in the Continental Army was not unusual from 1777 onward, there is no way to tell exactly what Freeman's role was during his service. Some Blacks fought on the battlefield, some served behind the lines in noncombatant roles (cooks, waiters, valets, etc.) and some served in the Navy. In Freeman's pension application, the section for "battles fought in" is blank, which may indicate that he served behind the lines rather than in them.

While Freeman said he served as a cook and/or a waiter to General George Washington, there is no evidence to prove or disprove the fact. However, it is known that Washington brought his personal cook and valet with him to the war from Mount Vernon, so it is unlikely that Freeman served General Washington as he claimed. What seems more likely is that Freeman was a cook and/or a waiter during the war and that one or more times he cooked for or served the commanding general. Perhaps the truth that Freeman "cooked for" Washington later became the story

5. Plymouth Freeman's Revolutionary War discharge papers. The papers, signed by George Washington, show that Freeman enlisted in the army in 1777, served until his discharge in 1783, and received the Badge of Merit for six years' service. Courtesy of the National Archives and Records Administration.

that he "was the cook for" Washington. Either way, Freeman served in the Continental Army for six years—a laudable act in itself—until he was discharged on June 8, 1783, and mustered out at West Point, New York. Upon his discharge, he received the Badge of Merit for his six years of service in the army. Where he went from West Point is unknown.

Ten years later, Freeman was issued his one-hundred-acre land bounty for his war service. The land was part of a four-thousand-acre tract in the US Military District of Ohio in the Northwest Territory. Federal land warrant records show that Freeman sold his land to speculator John Rathbone, who made a fortune purchasing and then reselling land bounties from Revolutionary War veterans. Veterans typically sold their land bounties at this time, having no interest in making the arduous—and dangerous—move to the Ohio territory that was still inhabited by Native Americans fighting to keep their homelands.

It is unclear when Freeman came to Cazenovia, but he is listed in the 1800 and 1820 censuses for Cazenovia and Nelson, respectively, while some historians claim Freeman lived in the town of Smithfield in 1808 and 1814. However, Freeman did live in Cazenovia in 1806–9, according to newspaper notices and local records. The ledgers for Samuel Forman's dry goods store have multiple entries for "P. Freeman, Sr., negro" from no. 1 town (Nelson) for 1806–7. The entries show that Freeman purchased items such as tools, clothing, whiskey, molasses, and other "sundries," for which he paid not in cash but through trade and labor. The Forman ledgers show Freeman paid his debts with bushels of wheat, by work "in haying," and by unspecified "work." Apparently, Freeman would also work for other people in the town who would sometimes pay his store bills. In the Lorenzo State Historic Site archives is a note and personal check from Jedediah Jackson to Samuel Forman, September 21, 1806, stating, "Please pay the bearer, Plymouth Freeman, 21 shillings and 9 pence out of your store and charge the same to me."

Other proof of Freeman's residence in Cazenovia is found in the pages of the *Cazenovia Pilot*, the earliest newspaper in the village, which listed the residents who had letters left in the post office for them to pick up. Seven such listings for Plymouth Freeman are found between October 1808 and July 1809. It is interesting that Freeman had letters waiting for him in the post office considering that existing documents suggest he could not write (although perhaps he could read).

Freeman lived as a farmer, and had a wife and at least one child, his son Jeremiah (Crane's childhood friend "black Jerry"). Jeremiah was born in 1805 and, according to an April 1807 letter in the Cazenovia Public Library historic archives, Jeremiah's mother—whom the letter calls "a Negroe woman the wife of old Plymouth"—was among several people in the Cazenovia area who had recently died. (No records exist that name Plymouth Freeman's wife, and even Jeremiah's death record in Battle Creek, Michigan, in 1886 states his mother's name as "unknown.")

In April 1818, Plymouth Freeman, age seventy-six, being "in need of the assistance of his bounty for support," applied for his government pension to which he was entitled for having served in the Revolutionary War. His application to receive the pension of eight dollars per month was signed and approved by Madison County Judge William Whipple, and four months later certified in the Madison County Clerk's Office by Deputy Clerk William Jarvis Hough (another famous Cazenovian—see his chapter later in this book). Freeman's pension was issued May 4, 1819, at which time he was paid $135.69 to make up for his thirteen-month wait.

According to the *Utica Tribune*, Freeman also lived at some point in the settlement of New Guinea, a village founded by free Blacks about one mile north of the village of Chittenango on the road toward North Manlius. The report states that the village of New Guinea was actually named in honor of Plymouth Freeman, who claimed to have been kidnapped from Guinea, Africa, as a child and "claimed to have been George Washington's waiter."

Plymouth Freeman died on August 25, 1829, at age eighty-seven, and was buried "in the small cemetery near where he had lived" in New Guinea. Freeman's son Jeremiah continued to live in the Central New York area, first in Chittenango and then in DeWitt. He married and had five children, owned his own house, owned multiple parcels of land, and was, by all appearances, living well and successfully. In October 1879, Jeremiah was mentioned in a Syracuse *Daily Journal* newspaper article as presiding over a meeting of the First African Methodist Episcopal Church as its oldest male member. Less than one year later, in September 1880, Freeman was drawn to serve as a grand juror for the Onondaga County court—the first time in the history of the county that a Black man was selected for a jury. "Mr. Freeman is an industrious and respected citizen, and a man of intelligence," according to the Syracuse *Daily Courier*.

MADISON COUNTY, ss.

On this _6th_ day of , _April_ 181_8_ , before me the subscriber, one of the Judges of the court of common pleas of the county of Madison aforesaid, personally appears _Plymouth Freeman_ aged _Sixty_ years, resident in _Cazenovia_ in the said county, who being by me first duly sworn, according to law, doth, on his oath, make the following declaration, in order to obtain the provision made by the late act of congress, entitled "An act to provide for certain persons engaged in the land and naval service of the United States, in the revolutionary war;" That he the said _Plymouth_ enlisted in _May_ 1777 in the state of _Connecticut_ , in the company commanded by captain of the _8_ _Connecticut Regt._

that he continued to serve in the said corps, or in the service of the U. States until the _Eighth Day of June_ 1783

W H Point , when he was discharged from service in state of _New york_ , that he was in the battles of

and that he is in reduced circumstances, and stands in need of the assistance of his country for support; and that he has no other evidence now in his power of said services.

Built in Exchange _Plymouth Freeman_

Sworn to and declared before me, the day and year aforesaid.

William Whipple Judge Madison Com Pleas

I, _William Whipple_ , Judge, &c. as aforesaid, do certify, that it appears to my satisfaction, that the said _Plymouth Freeman_ did serve in the revolutionary war, as stated in the preceding declaration, against the common enemy; and I now transmit the proceedings and testimony taken and had before me, to the Secretary for the department of War, pursuant to the directions of the aforementioned act of Congress.

Cazenovia April 6th 1818 _William Whipple_

State of New York Madison,
County Clerks Office } ss. I certify that it appears of record in this office that William Whipple Esq was a Judge of the Court of Common Pleas in & for the County of Madison duly commissioned qualified on the 6 th day of April last and that his signature to the above are in his hand writing. In Testimony whereof I have hereunto put my name & affixed the Seal of said Court this 10 th day of August 1818 —
Wm Jarvis Hough Dep. Clk

6. Plymouth Freeman's pension award, completed in 1818 by Madison County Judge (and Cazenovia resident) William Whipple and filed by Assistant County Clerk (and also Cazenovia resident) William Jarvis Hough. Courtesy of the National Archives and Records Administration.

Jeremiah Freeman died September 10, 1885, in Battle Creek, Michigan. His death record for Calhoun County, Michigan, states that he died of typhoid fever, that he was a mulatto, that his father's name was Plymouth and his mother's name was unknown, and that his father's occupation was that he "worked for Gen. Washington who set him free and gave him his name."

In the Shadow of Abolition

The Unknown Lives of the Johnson Family,
Slaves to Cazenovia's Founding Father

At times, a progressive spirit has swept the nation and Cazenovia has frequently been in the forefront of the movement. Whether temperance, women's rights, or, more recently, agribusiness, citizens of Cazenovia are and always have been progressively minded. Perhaps no issue has ignited the zeal of Cazenovians like the fight for abolition in the nineteenth century. As such, the village was the appropriate setting for the now-famous Anti-fugitive Slave Law Convention of 1850. Frederick Douglass, Gerrit Smith, and the Edmonson sisters, among others, convened in the village for two days, during which time they advocated for the immediate abolition of slavery and condoned the use of violence in efforts to help enslaved individuals escape bondage. This event highlighted Cazenovia as a center of humanitarianism and freethinking ideals for years to come.

It is ironic, then, that according to the John Jay College of Criminal Justice's records of Enslaved Persons, merely forty years earlier there were twelve slaves living in the village and thirty-five within Madison County. Worse, the owners were some of Cazenovia's most revered founding fathers, including John Lincklaen, Samuel Foreman, and Perry Childs. The Lorenzo State Historic Site in Cazenovia has kept excellent records throughout the two-hundred-year history of the estate, and its archives hold clues about the lives of one family of slaves who were brought to Cazenovia.

In 1798, just five years after establishing the village of Cazenovia, John Lincklaen purchased from his father-in-law General Benjamin Ledyard an eleven-year-old child named Caesar Johnson for $150.87. Two of

7. Attendees at the Anti-fugitive Slave Law Convention in Cazenovia, 1850. Near the center of the photograph are Frederick Douglass and Mary and Emily Edmonson. Courtesy of the J. Paul Getty Museum, Los Angeles. Digital image courtesy of the Getty's Open Content Program.

Caesar's siblings, Juliann and Titus Johnson, were also listed as slaves at the Lorenzo estate on the 1810 census. The Johnson siblings and their father had been owned by the Ledyard family for many years and were brought to Cazenovia by Benjamin's daughter Helen when she married John Lincklaen in 1797. Four-year-old Titus had been presented to Helen as a gift that same year, perhaps on the occasion of her marriage.

The Johnson children enslaved at Lincklaen's estates (Willowbank and later Lorenzo) were three of the six born to Pero Johnson of Middletown Point, New Jersey. Records pertaining to the siblings are scant and little is known about their duties. It is known that Caesar served John Lincklaen as a valet and it is assumed that Titus and Juliann, ages four and seven, respectively, when they came to Cazenovia, would have held similar domestic household positions, perhaps involving help in the kitchen. Slaves held on northern estates like Lorenzo were high-status property kept to bolster the sophisticated reputations of their owners, and it is unlikely they were used for manual labor. According to documents at Lorenzo, the siblings were lodged, along with two white servants, in rooms above the kitchen, with a staircase leading to the floor below.

The Johnson siblings' time at Lorenzo was not without incident, however. Following John Lincklaen's death in 1822, an estate inventory item—listed between a tea tray and a bank notation—notes an eleven-year-old mulatto child living at Lorenzo named Harriet Lincklaen, "never having been considered by her late master or her mistress in the light exactly of a slave." Her birth in 1811 coincided with a time in which both Juliann Johnson (age twenty-one) and Jonathan Ledyard (age eighteen), Helen Lincklaen's younger brother and John Lincklaen's partner and heir (who later took the last name "Lincklaen"), were both living at the estate. While there is no concrete proof Juliann and Jonathan were involved, the two were nearly the same age and it is possible Harriet was a product of their relationship. Further evidence comes from documents unearthed by former Lorenzo site manager Russell Grills under forgotten stacks of land contracts in an attic trunk at the estate. An 1832 letter from the Poormaster of nearby Lafayette to Jonathan Ledyard requests one hundred dollars for the maintenance of one Harriet "Linking" (then age twenty-one) and her illegitimate child. The payment points strongly to a sense of responsibility toward the young woman; whether it was financial or paternal hasn't been proved. It certainly would not have been

8. Lorenzo, the family home of John Lincklaen, founder of Cazenovia, was built in 1807 and was the home to the Johnson family for most of their enslavement in Cazenovia. The house still stands today at the southern end of Cazenovia Lake. It is now a New York State Historic Park. Photo by Jason Emerson.

unusual at the time for Jonathan Ledyard to produce a child with a slave, although modern sensibilities cannot help but feel outrage at the plight of any young woman held in bondage forced to bear the attentions of her master's family. Whether or not Juliann and Jonathan were Harriet's parents remains a mystery. A genteel veil has since been pulled across the episode when discussing the Cazenovia founding family's history—and it has seldom been mentioned since.

The first decade of the nineteenth century would prove to be an unstable time for Juliann's brother Titus as well. Sometime in the fifteen years between the Johnsons' arrival in Cazenovia and 1812, Titus was sold or loaned out on indenture to Dr. John H. Frisbee of Camillus, over thirty miles away. This separation must have been a considerable hardship for the three children, as they had no way of visiting each other and no control over their destinies. Then in 1812, at the age of nineteen, Titus was sold by Frisbee's widow to Perry Childs. Childs, a prominent Cazenovia attorney, was married to Helen Lincklaen's sister, Catherine, who also owned James Johnson, Titus's younger brother. This change in fortune would reunite Titus with his sibling, which must have come as a welcome turn to the young men.

New York State abolished slavery beginning in 1827. Many owners, including the Ledyards and Lincklaens, had foreseen this eventuality and worked to prepare their slaves for freedom. According to a letter written by General Ledyard to Helen Lincklaen in 1800, he encouraged her "to procure them to be taught within the first ten years to read intelligently the plain English languages." This provision proved prescient because manumission before 1827 would only be granted if the enslaved person could meet certain criteria: having attained literacy or two years of schooling, and having reached the age of twenty-five. The condescension with which Ledyard describes the children is breathtaking to modern eyes, however. In indenture papers for Caesar and Juliann of the same year, General Ledyard writes, "I had always intended at a future time to emancipate and let free the said children, if their conduct in the early part of life should merit it, and appearances should be in favor of their well-doing for themselves and society, and to which I fondly hoped might be the case by or before the period of time should arrive, which would make them twenty-five years of age; this too not less because I have been totally disappointed in a similar expectation in favor of their father Pero, who has cost me a great deal of expense and trouble from his infancy in endeavoring to make him capable of his own master and a good Member of Society and all in vain."

That slaves should have to prove they can be their own master speaks to the deep racism that pervaded the mindsets of many people in both the North and South at this period in history. And yet, six years ahead of the state abolition deadline, Perry Childs freed his slave Titus Johnson on April 18, 1821. Childs may also have conferred a settlement upon the twenty-eight-year-old man to help assist him in his new life.

Titus apparently was married at age fourteen, in 1807, to a child named Hannah, herself only nine years old, according to Supreme Court records for the state of Connecticut. Hannah, originally from Huntington, Connecticut, was an indentured servant at the time to a man in Cazenovia and it is presumed theirs was an arranged marriage, which would remain unconsummated until the parties reached maturity. In 1819, Titus visited Hannah and they were able to live as a married couple for a year before Titus was required to return to Cazenovia. The couple's time together produced a son, Richard, who was born in 1820. Court records do not state whether Titus visited Hannah on a trip with Mr. Childs or whether he was granted leave to visit her alone. It is illustrative of the slave experience that Titus presumably had little choice in his marriage, nor was he able to live with his wife without the consent of his master. Records do not mention Titus visiting his wife and son again. He passed away in Cazenovia in 1826 at the age of thirty-three, just five years after gaining his freedom.

Titus's name would go on, however, linked to the 1851 Connecticut Supreme Court case *New Haven vs. Huntington* that contained legislation regarding the property rights of slaves. The town of Huntington brought suit on behalf of Titus's widow Hannah, her daughter-in-law Sybil, and Hannah's three illegitimate children. It was alleged that the settlement conferred on Titus by Perry Childs should be inherited by Titus's grandchildren and their relations in order to support the family. The court maintained that Titus's status as a slave at the time of his son Richard's birth should not preclude him or other heirs from inheritance. However, it was also decided that the town of Huntington, and not Child's settlement on Titus, should maintain Hannah because this is where she and the children resided. It was a landmark case and would certainly have had repercussions in the tumultuous years preceding the Civil War.

No manumission records have been located for either Caesar, Juliann, James, or Frank, another of the Johnson siblings living in Cazenovia. This is not particularly surprising, however, because New York did not require manumission records to be held by the town except at the freedman's request. Those that chose to preserve copies may have done so as protection against reenslavement and it is significant that none of the other Johnsons chose to record them. Juliann, also listed as "July Ann" in the Cazenovia newspaper the *Pilot*, was living in Cazenovia as late as the 1820s, where she is listed among those with mail at the post office on numerous occasions throughout the early part of the decade. By that date, she would have reached the age of emancipation (twenty-five) as well as presumably learned to read "the plain English languages," as in the conditions laid out in the 1799 New York Abolition law. It can be assumed she was a free woman of Cazenovia by 1820.

Records on Caesar, James, and Frank have not been located, except for a listing in Evergreen Cemetery for Frank, buried in the potter's field on December 19, 1820, when he was just thirty years old. In a biographical document known as CazFolk, compiled and frequently updated by Cazenovia historians, there are numerous Johnsons identified as Black living in Cazenovia during the late nineteenth and early twentieth centuries. And while the name Johnson is not uncommon, the limited number of African Americans in the village makes it likely these were descendants of the Johnson siblings.

The African American experience in Cazenovia has been spottily documented but there is reason to hope that newly digitized archives may help unlock many of their untold stories. The surviving Johnson siblings were all emancipated by 1827 at the latest, and it does not take much imagination to place them at the momentous events of the 1850 Anti-fugitive Slave Law Convention in the heart of the Cazenovia village. Many of the speakers over the two-day convention had witnessed slavery in the northeast firsthand. Abolitionist Gerrit Smith grew up working among slaves near Cazenovia and the experience crystalized the progressive views that would shape his later life. Frederick Douglass was himself held in bondage in Maryland and would have been one of the few people present that day who could directly empathize with the Johnsons' experiences.

We may never know if the Johnsons attended the convention or what they thought at the time. But it is clear that fifty years after the children were brought to Cazenovia as slaves, the views of the village and nation had changed profoundly. With few exceptions, Cazenovians identified with the antislavery Republican party, and, as the 1850s wore on, with the cause of abolition as well. The village would become a stop on the Underground Railroad as well as a pulpit from which abolitionist leaders expounded their views. It can only be hoped that Juliann, Caesar, or James were present to share in the cause of freedom.

Jonathan Forman

With Washington through the Revolution and after

While Samuel Forman is typically recognized by Cazenovians as one of the two founders of the community (along with John Lincklaen), his older brother, Jonathan Forman, is less well known. Jonathan, however, was not only one of the leading citizens of Cazenovia before his death in 1809, but he also earned a distinguished record serving in the Revolutionary War under generals Washington, Lafayette, and Sullivan and, later, marching with President Washington to suppress the 1894 Whiskey Rebellion in Pennsylvania.

According to Helen Lincklaen Fairchild, a Forman family descendant, Jonathan and Samuel Forman were among the children of Judge Samuel Forman and Helen Denise, of New Jersey. Jonathan, instilled by his father with a sincere patriotism, walked away from his studies at Princeton College at age nineteen and joined the New Jersey militia in 1775 as a lieutenant at the start of the American Revolution. In December 1776, he was commissioned a captain in the New Jersey Continental Line and served with distinction throughout the war. "He fought in every engagement where Washington commanded, sharing the privations of the winter camp at Valley Forge and the triumph of the surrender of Lord Cornwallis at Yorktown," Fairchild wrote.

Forman served with General John Sullivan on the expedition against the Six Nations in Pennsylvania and New York in the summer of 1779, then was promoted to the rank of major for his valor and transferred to a battalion of light artillery in Virginia under General LaFayette, under whom he served at the battle of Yorktown. Forman spent the next few years stationed in New York State. He was promoted to lieutenant colonel in the Second New Jersey Regiment in 1783 and was retained in the New Jersey Battalion. At the end of the war, Forman left the army with the rank of colonel, although, according to his family, he also left with "broken health and fortunes."

Forman married Mary Ledyard of Groton, Connecticut, and had two daughters, one of whom died at ten months old. The family lived on a farm in Middle Point, New Jersey, and opened a general store in the town. In 1794, Forman was recalled to military service to command the Third Infantry Regiment of New Jersey—with the army personally led by President George Washington—to help quash the Whiskey Rebellion in Pennsylvania. "Left out from home having Mrs. Forman ill with the fever, and myself very unwell," the thirty-nine-year-old Forman wrote in the journal he kept of the march into Pennsylvania. According to Forman's daughter, Mary Forman Seymour, when Washington saw her father during the march he said, "Colonel Forman! Always the first in the field." Forman's journal stated that he personally met with President Washington to explain an incident that occurred during the march and he also dined with the president during the trip. "Nothing remarkable," he wrote of the dinner in his journal, in the understated tone of a frequent acquaintance. (On the other hand, Major William Gould, who was invited to the dinner along with Forman and another officer, wrote in his journal: "Accepted an invitation from the President to take a glass of wine with him, after which dined very agreeably.")

In 1796, Forman, with his wife and daughter, moved to Cazenovia (then a community only three years old). According to the Forman family historian, when the colonel and his family traveled to Upstate New York, "It is said that there was then no carriage road and in many places they were obliged to use axes to make their way in that direction. It is said that the carriage of Colonel Forman was the first conveyance of the kind that passed beyond the site of Whitestown. He drove to Chittenango, and the family went thence to Cazenovia on horseback." In Cazenovia, Forman lived with his brother, Major Samuel S. Forman, and family. (The village censuses for 1800–1803 show them listed together, apparently considered one family of eight or nine total residents on thirty-eight total acres of land between two plots. The 1800 federal census also includes that Jonathan Forman owned three slaves while he was a Cazenovia resident.) Jonathan Forman was a storekeeper in Cazenovia (unsuccessfully, according to family tradition), served as a judge on the court of common pleas in 1800 and as a state assemblyman in 1800–1801, and was appointed a brigadier general in the state militia by Governor John Jay.

From 1801 to 1802, Forman was directly involved in a militia dispute that ultimately caused the governor's involvement and became statewide news when every militia officer in the Chenango County regiment (there was no Madison County yet formed in 1801) of the fifth military division of the state—including Cazenovia town founder and militia lieutenant colonel John Lincklaen—resigned their commissions. In early 1801, Lieutenant Colonel Benjamin Hovey, of the Chenango County regiment, refused to hold a military parade ordered by the outgoing Federalist governor, John Jay. Hovey, a Democratic Republican, was accused of "openly and intentionally violating" the order from the militia commander in chief, and for neglecting his duty and "publicly disobeying and condemning" Brigadier General Jonathan Forman's orders of April 20, which instructed Hovey to follow the governor's prior orders.

Hovey was arrested and court-martialed by order of General Forman, and ultimately removed from office. Hovey appealed the decision to the new governor, George Clinton, a Democratic Republican who also happened to be an old friend and mentor. Governor Clinton's decision on the appeal, on December 16, 1801, overturned Hovey's court martial for lack of evidence and reinstated Hovey to his position. Clinton's decision also rebuked Brigadier General Forman, stating that five officer appointments he had made to the brigade, also in April 1801, were "injurious to the service, unauthorized by law, and inconsistent with the constitution of the state." On January 28, 1802, Clinton removed Forman from the militia for "illegally assuming the power of appointing." Clinton ultimately replaced Forman with the newly promoted Brigadier General Hovey.

Nineteen officers of the Chenango County regiment—many of whom were leading citizens of Cazenovia, including Colonel John Lincklaen, Major Samuel S. Forman, and Lieutenant Elisha Farnham—were so outraged by the governor's decisions that they resigned their military commissions en masse on February 3, 1802, and published their group resignation letter to the governor in the New York newspapers. The letter stated that General Forman's removal "has excited in their breasts the most lively emotions of indignation and regret," and the governor's decision to reverse Hovey's court martial and restore the rank of a man who "willfully and notoriously" disobeyed orders and defied his commanders was so repugnant to their honor, that they were compelled to resign. The mass resignation was widely covered in the state press, but the governor was unmoved by the gesture; the officers were allowed to resign and never readmitted to the militia.

Forman stayed on in Cazenovia, one of the small community's most respected residents. Years later, Colonel Charles D. Miller told a story about the old Revolutionary War veteran who was not, apparently, one to frequent the church. According to the story, Forman was persuaded by Presbyterian Reverend Joshua Leonard to attend the meeting house one day, after which he went to the village tavern. He "told his friends the persuasions the Elder had used with him. And the result? 'Well, I went,' replied the general in painful admission of his weakness, 'And when I got back the damned hens had scratched my garden all to pieces.'" Forman left Cazenovia after his wife's death in 1806 and moved in with his daughter Mary and son-in-law Henry Seymour (originally of Utica) in their home in Pompey Hill, a few miles away. Mary Forman Seymour had six children, one of whom was Horatio Seymour, later governor of New York.

Jonathan Forman died in his daughter's home in 1809. "He was a man of singularly warm and tender heart, and much beloved, and famous for his sense of fun," according to his granddaughter, Helen Fairchild. One history of Madison County said Forman was "energetic in forming the old Military Brigade of Madison County, and was always prominent at parades, having a true soldierly bearing." In 1825, during the Marquis de Lafayette's tour of America, Forman's daughter traveled to Utica to meet the famous Revolutionary War general. "I was a young girl at the time," stated her daughter, Mary Forman Seymour Miller, "and when my mother wished to take me with her to Mrs. Johnson's to be introduced to Lafayette, I foolishly thought it would be far more interesting to see the procession from the top of a building on Genesee Street . . . than to go to the reception, and how often have I deeply regretted my decision. My mother was much overcome at meeting the general and could scarcely command her voice to ask him if he remembered her father, but he instantly recalled him as having been one of his lieutenants at Valley Forge."

Jonathan Forman was buried with his wife Mary in Evergreen Cemetery in Cazenovia.

1816

The Year without a Summer

Throughout much of the world, 1816 is known as the "Year without a Summer" or the "Poverty Year." The massive 1815 eruption of Mount Tambora on the island of Sumbawa, Indonesia, in combination with the tail end of the "Little Ice Age," set in motion a volcanic winter event that would have disastrous consequences throughout the northern hemisphere. Tambora's eruption spewed tons of ash and aerosol particles into the atmosphere. As they dispersed into the stratosphere, the particles traveled around the globe, blocking the sun and dropping the global temperature approximately three to six degrees Fahrenheit; a catastrophe for the world below. The American northeast was particularly hard hit by unseasonably cold weather throughout the growing season, destroying crops and leading to famine and disease in the months that followed.

Newspapers throughout the northeast documented the astonishment and dismay felt by farmers and townspeople alike at the prospect of a growing season cut off before it began. The *Boston Gazette* of August 19, 1816, noted, "Much alarm existed in this county in the early part of July as to the coming in of the harvest. So extremely and unusually cold was the weather, it was apprehended that there would be a great scarcity of hay and bread the ensuing year." If commercial centers like those of Boston were concerned with the harvest, rural societies throughout New York were more anxious still. In a tone of considerable alarm, the *Geneva Gazette* of June 12 exclaimed: "Winter in June! During the past week the weather has been extremely cold for the season, and we have experienced several severe frosts, which have nearly destroyed the gardens and done much injury to the crops of grain. On Thursday morning a considerable quantity of SNOW fell." In Canandaigua, the *Ontario Repository* of June 11 remarked that "Some of our farmers are planting their corn a second time; and our gardens, especially in fruit and vines, have suffered much from frost and drought."

For many eking out a living in the hardscrabble rural north, a lost harvest could mean the difference between survival and starvation. In Ashland, New Hampshire, Reuben Whitten managed to grow just enough wheat to share with his neighbors that year, and when he passed away in 1847, they erected a monument in his honor which read, "A pioneer of this town. Cold season of 1816 raised 40 bushils of wheat on this land whitch kept his family and neighbours from starveation." The year 1816 would prove to be one of extreme adversity for many, and tragedy for some.

Cazenovia was not exempt from the privations of that year. In a business letter dated August 9, Cazenovia's founder John Lincklaen wrote to his friend and attorney Paul Busti: "I have some expectations of being favored before this time with a visit from Mr. —— and Mr. Van Staphorst, but perhaps the extraordinary coldness of the season may have deterred them from undertaking so long a journey." The shortage in oats, and resulting price inflation, raised the cost of keeping horses and made the prospect of long-distance travel very costly. Lincklaen, despite his status as a wealthy elite, would have been concerned by the climate emergency befalling his community. His fortunes were tied to the success of the Cazenovia venture, and with crops failing and prospective settlers eyeing warmer, western lands, he would have taken the situation seriously.

Cazenovia's original newspaper, the *Pilot*, of Wednesday, June 12, 1816, included a brief account of the weather that summer. It stands out for its mention of daily conditions rather than politics and land sales, which tended to dominate the news of the day: "Perhaps at no period has been witnessed so lengthy and so severe cold weather at this season of the year. Vegetation which but a few days ago appeared in her gayest attire, now stands dressed in the sable habiliments of mourning. From the first to the tenth winds from the northwest and frost, we believe, every night. On the sixth a severe snow storm, which continued with but little intermission for eight or ten hours. Since the tenth the weather has become more mild, and prospects more flattering to the 'husband-man.'"

The year without a summer and its effects loomed large in the collective memory of the residents. In 1885, Henry Severance recalled in his reminiscences, "For the whole season of 1816 . . . we well remember the gravest apprehensions were felt by all for the consequences incident to such a general loss of crops, and the prospects of famine in the near future." At various times, the *Cazenovia Republican* has revisited the event, calling readers to remember and reflect on a year when Mother Nature turned her back on this fair village.

In 1916, on the one-hundredth anniversary of the summerless year, *Republican* editor J. C. Peck compared the relatively mild winter experienced that year with that of a century before:

> The summer of 1816 was regarded as one of exceptional cold. Snow fell in May and June, something practically unknown before or since. This unseasonable weather was double hardship because the people had just about recovered from the War of 1812 and were endeavoring to develop the country. It is recorded that there was a heavy frost as late as June 9, 1816.
>
> Want was general and hardship was felt by all classes. Provisions were very high, the price of flour at one time being $16.

The *Cazenovia Republican* of 1939 once again revived the memory of "Eighteen Hundred and Froze to Death," as it came to be called, and its effect on Cazenovia and the surrounding region. At that time, Cazenovians were facing another threat, this time manmade, and could look back at their ancestors' fortitude in the face of hardship to steel themselves for the possible conflict brewing in Europe. In the March 9, 1939, edition, Cazenovia Town Historian Jabez W. Abell wrote:

> Is it not a little surprising that for the whole season of 1816, called the year without a summer, and when the greatest apprehensions were felt by all for the consequences incident to such a general loss of crops and the prospect of famine in the near future, they did not, like the Second Adventists, prepare their ascension robes to go aloft in, but they did at this very time, with want and famine staring them in the face, prepare to construct the Erie Canal.

Abell went on to chronicle the effects of the weather on the areas surrounding Cazenovia. If residents were to survive the year, they would need to sell and trade with larger cities around them. Nowhere in the region was spared the effects of the volcanic winter, however.

From Young's *History of Chautauqua County,* we extract the following:

"The cold summer of 1816, though not confined to Chautauqua county, is deemed worthy of record. The writer well remembers planting corn the sixth day of June in a snowstorm in the eastern part of the state, and can add his testimony to that of thousands who have declared it to be the coldest season they have ever known. Persons are in the habit of speaking of the summer of 1816, as the coldest ever known in America or Europe."

According to Abell's research, the winter preceding the disastrous summer was relatively mild. It was only as summer approached that the population became anxious as conditions worsened.

April began warm, and grew colder as the month advanced, and ended with snow and ice, with a temperature more like winter than spring.

May was more remarkable for its frowns than smiles, buds and fruits were frozen, ice formed half an inch in thickness, corn was killed and the fields were planted again and again until it was considered too late.

June was the coldest ever known in this latitude. Frost, ice and snow were common, snow fell to the depth of ten inches in Vermont and Maine and three inches in the interior of New York state.

July was accompanied by frost and ice. On the morning of the Fourth, ice formed of the thickness of window glass throughout New England, New York, and Pennsylvania.

August was more cheerless if possible than the summer months already passed. Ice was formed half an inch in thickness, almost every green thing was destroyed in this county and in Europe.

September furnished about two weeks of the mildest weather of the season. Soon after the middle it became very cold and frosty, ice forming a quarter of an inch in thickness.

Cazenovia of the early 1800s had been riding a wave of prosperity. With the cessation of hostilities after the War of 1812, new settlers from the east arrived in record numbers, driving the price of land to an all-time high of twelve dollars per acre (approximately $120 per acre in 2018). New industry, in the form of timber and grist mills and clock and cabinet manufacturers, flourished along the Chittenango Creek and Cazenovia's future seemed assured. However, the effects of the volcanic winter event of 1816 would presage challenging years ahead for the village as crops died, prices rose, and settlers chose warmer lands further west. The construction of the Erie Canal, and its bypass of Cazenovia, would only add to the hardships facing the village during the first half of the nineteenth century. And while Cazenovia would eventually innovate and evolve into a successful hamlet once more, 1816 would remain a watershed year, marking a time of trial for its robust and hardy citizens.

First Grammar Book of the Ojibwe Language Written and Published in Cazenovia

It is not only "famous" people who contribute to society or help change the world; it is, on the whole, regular everyday people who have an idea, work hard to bring it to fruition, then pass away into history. Their ideas and work remain to influence posterity, but they are often forgotten. One such contributor was a full-blooded Ojibwe (also called Chippeway) Native American named Sahgahjewagahbahweh who wrote and published the first grammar book of the Chippeway language in North America while he lived in Cazenovia to attend the local seminary in 1833–34.

Sahgahjewagahbahweh, also called John Summerfield, was born around the turn of the nineteenth century and was from the Canadian town of Mississauga, near Toronto, on the shores of Lake Ontario. His father, White John, was killed fighting with the British against America during the War of 1812. Sahgahjewagahbahweh lived in the Credit Mission, also known as the Credit Indian Village, which was founded with the help of the Methodist Missionary Society, and in which the native inhabitants had converted to Christianity. He was known as a bright youth and, at some point, came under the tutelage of Reverend William Case, a highly regarded Methodist minister and later superintendent of Indian Missions in Upper Canada.

Case saw potential in Sahgahjewagahbahweh, and worked to send the Ojibwe youth, along with two others of his tribe, to the Oneida Conference seminary in Cazenovia, New York, so the three could undertake a quality religious education. According to scholar Donald B. Smith, a group of young women in New York City, aged ten to fifteen, collected forty dollars to pay Sahgahjewagahbahweh's school fees, while a second group of Methodists in New York City raised more money to supplement those funds. The Mississauga youth, in addition to funding, was also given an English name: John Summerfield. The "Young Ladies Society of John-street Church" chose the name to honor the late Reverend John Summerfield, a popular young Irish American evangelist and president of the young men's missionary society.

The village of Cazenovia was only forty years old when John Summerfield arrived in the fall of 1833. The community had about 240 dwellings, four churches (Presbyterian, Methodist, Baptist, and Congregational), three hotels, numerous mills and factories, ten dry goods stores, six grocery stores, a land office, a bookstore and bindery, a printing office and local newspaper, and the seminary established by the Methodist Oneida Conference in 1825. The seminary was located in the former county courthouse building, described at the time as "a substantial brick building standing on a conspicuous and beautiful location." Two buildings were added to the seminary before Summerfield's arrival, and two more, for dormitories and a dining hall, were erected the year he arrived.

Summerfield joined more than 250 students attending the seminary, both male and female. According to seminary historians, students in Cazenovia faced a rigorous regimen of work, prayers, and meals that went from 5 a.m. to 5 p.m. At meals, the boys sat on small backless stools on one side of a long, narrow oilcloth-covered table while the girls faced them on the other side. While the two sexes were allowed to study and eat together, they were not allowed to converse. The living quarters, according to a student in 1835, one year after Summerfield attended, were "so small [that] . . . ordinary bedsteads were out of the question. Instead thereof we had turnup bedsteads which when folded served as a wardrobe as well as a sleeping apparatus."

The courses at the seminary were those of a classical education: Latin, Greek, algebra, surveying, astronomy, chemistry, natural philosophy, bookkeeping, logic, French, rhetoric, and painting. According to Smith, the Ojibwe students loved "reading, especially biography and history." For exams, seminary students had to orally answer questions from their teachers as well as from any spectators in attendance. They also were examined by the entire board of trustees and board of visitors before they could receive their diplomas.

CAZENOVIA SEMINARY IN 1882.

9. Drawing of Cazenovia Seminary as it looked in 1832, when John Summerfield was a student there. Originally printed in the book *First Fifty Years of Cazenovia Seminary, 1825–1875*, published in 1877. Public domain image.

During his year in Cazenovia, Summerfield composed a thirty-five-page booklet that was the first grammar ever written of the Ojibwe language. He completed this project, in the midst of all his studies, "as an exercise for my leisure hours . . . during the past winter," he wrote in the advertisement at the front of the booklet. Apparently, some of his friends were so impressed by his work that they encouraged him to have it printed, which he did, "by a fellow student, at his own suggestion and expense." Summerfield's book, *Sketch of Grammar of the Chippeway Language, to which is Added a Vocabulary of Some of the Most Common Words*, was published by Cazenovia printer J. F. Fairchild and Son in April 1834. The book, unsurprisingly, was no bestseller but, to this day, nearly two hundred years later, any book that studies the Ojibwe people or language refers to Summerfield's work as the first and one of the essential sources on the subject.

Unfortunately, Summerfield's bright star did not shine for long after he left Cazenovia as a seminary graduate. He was asked by the American

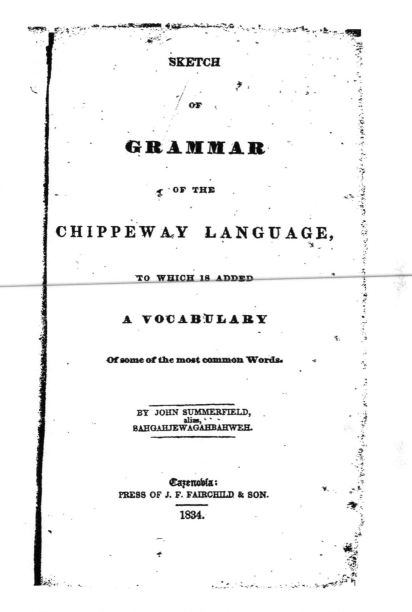

SKETCH

OF

GRAMMAR

OF THE

CHIPPEWAY LANGUAGE,

TO WHICH IS ADDED

A VOCABULARY

Of some of the most common Words.

BY JOHN SUMMERFIELD,
alias,
SAHGAHJEWAGAHBAHWEH.

Cazenovia:
PRESS OF J. F. FAIRCHILD & SON.

1834.

10. Title page of John Summerfield's grammar book of the Chippeway language, which he wrote while a student at Cazenovia Seminary and was published in Cazenovia in 1834. Public domain image.

Methodists to direct their educational program among the Menominee First Nations near Green Bay on Lake Michigan. Before he could take up the appointment, however, John Summerfield, "alias Sahgahjewagah-bahweh," died of tuberculosis at the Credit Mission. He was only thirty years old.

A History of Heartbreak

Who Was "Crazy Luce"?

In a 225-year-old community such as Cazenovia, folk tales, myths, and legends abound. One of the most famous and well-known stories in local history is the story of "Crazy Luce"—Lucy Dutton—a young woman who went insane and wandered the county for thirty years after her fiancé jilted her on her wedding day to marry her sister. But the story of Crazy Luce is not a tale whose interest is confined to Cazenovia. A database search of historical newspapers has shown that the touchstone telling of Lucy's sad tale, which dates to April 1847, was published dozens of times over a twenty-year period in newspapers throughout New York State and across the country. It found particular favor with newspaper editors and readers during the 1860s, especially during the Civil War.

Lucy's story continues to be remembered and retold to this day, at least in Upstate New York, and a state historic marker was even erected to her memory in Cazenovia in 2015.

Why has Lucy Dutton's story resonated through so many years and generations? It is difficult to say, but perhaps it is simply because Lucy's tale of heartbreak and insanity—coupled with a community's continuous caring for such a harmlessly pathetic and deranged individual—is so universal. Amid the fascination of Lucy's legend itself and its reach beyond the borders of Cazenovia and New York, a search for its history has uncovered something even more interesting—the story is even older than has been understood, and the original telling is not the same as the story we all know.

The Story of Crazy Luce

Lucy Dutton's story dates to the turn of the nineteenth century (different tellings offer different dates: 1800, 1802, and 1808 are the most prevalent), when Cazenovia was a young village, around one decade old, as were its surrounding communities. The story, famously written for posterity and published as "A Night of Years" in 1847 by Mrs. Sara Jane (Clarke) Lippincott, under the pen name Grace Greenwood, is as follows:

In 1807, Lucy Dutton, age nineteen, the daughter of a respectable farmer, lived in Cazenovia with her family, which included her parents and her younger sister Ellen. Both daughters were attractive and more intelligent and educated than most girls in the area. While Lucy was "winningly" beautiful, she was also serious, with a "nun-like serenity" that concealed a passionate nature. Ellen, on the other hand, was "strikingly" beautiful, impetuous, and spoiled.

Lucy became a schoolteacher in the village of Morrisville, and while there she met Edwin W——, a man of "excellent family and standing" in the town who was "handsome" with "some pretensions to fashion." The two fell in love and became engaged, after which they drove to Cazenovia to inform Lucy's parents. The Duttons gave their blessing to the union, and it was decided that Lucy would stay home in Cazenovia to prepare for the wedding in two months' time, on Lucy's twentieth birthday. Her sister Ellen would return to Morrisville with Edwin and take charge of Lucy's school for the remainder of the term.

Two months later, on a lovely May morning, neither the bridegroom nor the bride's sister appeared at the appointed time for the wedding ceremony. As evening started to fall—and hours later than expected—a carriage finally drove up containing the missing couple. Edwin was agitated, mentioned something about an "unavoidable delay," and then "stepping to the sideboard, tossed off a glass of wine, another, and another." He finally explained, after crossing the room to take Ellen's hand, that he could not undertake a marriage to Lucy, as he was already married to her sister. "I found that I had never loved until I knew your *second* daughter," Edwin supposedly told his new in-laws, explaining that he and Ellen had fallen in love over the past two months while Lucy was at home preparing for the wedding.

THE GOLDEN RULE

AND

ODD-FELLOWS' FAMILY COMPANION.

Popular Literature, Instruction and Amusement.

BY E. WINCHESTER. NEW-YORK, PHILADELPHIA AND BOSTON. TWO DOLLARS A-YEAR.

VOL. VI...No. 14. SATURDAY, APRIL 3, 1847. WHOLE No. 144.

Original Tales.

A NIGHT OF YEARS.

BY GRACE GREENWOOD.

MY READER: I have sat some minutes, with my pen suspended in air above my paper. I have been debating a delicate point—I am in a position. You will perhaps recollect that one of Fanny Forester's exquisite sketches was entitled "Lucy Dutton."

Now, it happens that the *real name* of the heroine of the "ower true tale" which I am about to do myself the honor of relating to you, was no other than Lucy Dutton. Shall I rob her of her birthright—compel her to wear a *nom de guerre*, because my sister-authoress accidentally gave the true name to one of her ideal creations? Shall I sacrifice truth to delicacy? that's the question. "No?" You said no, did you not? Then Lucy, Lucy Dutton, let it be.

Some forty years since, in the interior of my beautiful native State, New York, lived the father of our heroine, an honest and respectable farmer. He had but two children—Lucy, a noble girl of nineteen, and Ellen, a year or two younger. The first named was winningly, rather than strikingly beautiful. Under a manner observable for its seriousness, and nun-like serenity, were concealed an impassioned nature, and a heart of the deepest capacity for loving. She was remarkable from her earliest childhood for a voice of thrilling and haunting sweetness.

Ellen Dutton was the brilliant antipodes of her sister; a "born beauty," whose prerogative of prettiness was to have her irresponsible own way, in all things, and at all times. An indulgent father, a weak mother, and an idolizing sister, had all unconsciously contributed to the ruin of a nature not at the first remarkable for strength, or generosity.

Where, in all God's creatures, is heartlessness so seemingly unnatural—is selfishness so detestible, as in a beautiful woman?

Lucy possessed a fine intellect, and as her parents were well reared New Englanders, she and her sister were far better educated than from necessity. Thus, a few months previous to the commencement of our sketch, Lucy Dutton left for the first time her fire-side circle, to take charge of a school, some twenty miles form her native town.

For some while, her letters home were expressive only of the happy contentment which sprang from the consciousness of active usefulness, of receiving, while imparting good. But anon there came a change; then were those records for home, characterized by fitful gaiety, or dreary sadness; indefinable hopes and fears seemed striving for supremacy in the writer's troubled little heart. Lucy *loved*; but scarcely acknowledged it to herself, while she knew not that she was loved; so for a time, that beautiful second-birth of woman's nature was like a warm sunrise struggling with the cold mists of morning.

But one day brought a letter which could not soon be forgotten in the home of the absent one—a letter traced by a hand that trembled in sympathy with a heart tumultuous with happiness. Lucy had been wooed and won; and she but waited her parent's approval of her choice, to become the betrothed of young Edwin W——, a man of excellent family and standing in the town where she had been teaching. The father and mother accorded their sanction with many blessings, and Lucy's next letter promised a speedy visit from the lovers.

To such natures as Lucy's, what an absorbing, and yet what a revealing of self is a first passion—what a prodigality of giving, what an incalculable wealth of receiving—what a breaking up is there of the deep waters of the soul, and how heaven descends in a sudden star-shower upon life. If there is a season when an angel may look with intense and fearful interest upon her mortal sister, 'tis when she beholds her heart pass from the bud-like innocence and freshness of girlhood, and taking to its very core the fervid light of love, glow and crimson into perfect womanhood.

At last the plighted lovers came, and welcomes and festivities awaited them. Mr. W—— gave entire satisfaction to father, mother, and even to the exacting "beauty." He was a handsome man, with some pretensions to fashion; but in manner, and apparently in character, the opposite of his betrothed.

11. First page of "A Night of Years," Crazy Luce's story as it appeared in *The Odd-Fellow's Family Companion* in 1847. Public domain image.

According to Greenwood, Lucy heard the explanation with a strange calmness, then walked over and confronted her betrayers:

"As though to assure herself of the dread reality of the vision, she laid her hand on Ellen's shoulder, and let it glide down her arm—but she touched not Edwin. As those cold fingers met hers, the unhappy wife first gazed full into her sister's face; and as she marked the ghastly pallor of her cheek, the dilated nostril, the quivering lip, and the intensely mournful eyes, she covered her own face with her hands, and burst into tears, while the young husband, awed by the terrible silence of her he had wronged, gasped for breath, and staggered back against the wall. Then Lucy, clasping her hands on her forehead, first gave voice to her anguish and despair in one fearful cry, which could but ring forever through the souls of the guilty pair, and fell in a death-like swoon at their feet."

Lucy was unconscious for several hours, and when she awoke she was strangely silent. This silence continued for weeks until it was realized that she had become "hopelessly insane," although her madness was of a "mild and harmless nature." She sighed frequently, seemed burdened with a great sorrow, and had a great fear of men, all of whom she avoided. For the next thirty years, Lucy was a restless wanderer throughout Madison County, watched over by her parents until they died, then cared for and given places to sleep at the houses of caring friends and neighbors. "Through laughing springs and rosy summers, and golden autumns, and tempestuous winters, it was tramp, tramp, tramp; no rest for her of the crushed heart and the crazed brain," Greenwood wrote.

Greenwood, who stated that as a child she saw Lucy when she would sit by their family's hearth on many occasions, described her appearance as "very singular." Lucy's dress was a patchwork of different colors, her shawl was worn and torn, and in summer she would decorate her bonnet with picked flowers. She carried with her in a bundle whatever other clothing she possessed, as well as "a number of parcels of old rags, dried herbs, etc." Lucy also possessed a "torn and soiled" bible that she cherished.

According to Greenwood, Lucy only once spoke of her wedding day. When she met Greenwood's brother and asked him his name, he replied "William Edwin." Lucy "caught her hand away, and sighing heavily, said, as though thinking aloud, 'I knew an Edwin once, and he made me broken-hearted.'"

After three decades of wandering, Crazy Luce became ill and was taken in at the county almshouse. Her strength faded for a week, and then one morning she awoke with shockingly clear eyes and asked the matron where she was and where were Edwin and Ellen. Lucy said she had had a terrible dream that her fiancé and her sister had gotten married and she had been discarded on her wedding day. The matron told her it was not a dream, but all true—just at the moment that Lucy noticed her own hands that were no longer young, but "old and withered." The matron also told Lucy that her parents and sister were dead, and her former fiancé had moved away, far to the west.

"To the wretched Lucy, the last thirty years were all as though they had never been. Of not a scene, not an incident, had she the slightest remembrance, since the night when the recreant lover and the traitoress sister stood before her and made their terrible announcement," Greenwood wrote. Not long after these horrible revelations, Lucy Dutton passed away—"dead in her grey-haired youth!"

Greenwood's tale was published in her book, *Greenwood Leaves: A Collection of Sketches and Letters*, by Ticknor, Reed, and Fields in 1850, but was originally published as an article in *The Golden Rule* magazine in April 1847. Over the next several decades, the story was often reprinted in newspapers across the state and the country, as well as in multiple local history books. In addition to numerous retellings in the *Cazenovia Republican* (the first time appears to be in January 1856), a database search found Greenwood's story reprinted in 1847, 1857, 1862, 1865, 1866, 1869, and 1878 in newspapers such as the *Sacramento* [Calif.] *Daily Union*, the *Jeffersonian Democrat* [Chardon, OH], the *Bloomfield* [NJ] *Citizen*, the *Plattsburgh Sentinel*, the *Sag Harbor Express*, the *Chenango American*, the *Freeman's Journal* [Cooperstown, NY] and the *Troy Weekly Times*, among others.

Later Reminiscences and Retellings of Lucy's Tale

In addition to the repetitions of Lucy's sad story as related by Greenwood, there were also a number of Cazenovia-area and Upstate New York inhabitants who remembered her and wrote about her. Only weeks after Greenwood's story was originally published in April 1847, the editor of the *Eastern State Journal*, of White Plains, New York, reprinted Greenwood's story and offered his own memories of Lucy Dutton. The editor, Edmund G. Sutherland, grew up in Plymouth, New York, in Chenango County, and stated that he remembered Crazy Luce clearly and Greenwood's story was "true, almost literally."

Sutherland wrote that he had often seen Lucy wandering the streets of Chittenango, which was about forty miles from his hometown. "In 1832 was the last time we saw her," he wrote. "She was then an old woman. She wandered abroad, houseless, and homeless, and comfortless. The story of her early griefs we have often heard from the lips of those who were cognizant of the facts, and in our boyhood days shed a tear over the sorrows of that sad one, whose heart had been broken, and whose reason had been overthrown, by the circumstances which the narrative so accurately details."

Sutherland stated that he remembered Lucy as if it were yesterday: "She would often flee from the presence of a man, as a pure angel would avoid contact with an evil spirit. When she saw one in male attire coming toward her in the streets, she would invariably turn back, cross to the other side of the way, or climb a fence to take a circuit around and past him. Neither would she stay in a house overnight if she knew a man was under the same roof. Poor creature! She died in the Alms House at Cazenovia."

The Reverend Edward Mott Woolley, who grew up in Nelson Flats (present day hamlet of Nelson), wrote of Dutton in his 1855 memoir. "No matter how hungry and cold she might be, she would never enter our dwelling if father was there, for she possessed wonderful fear of men; but she would draw her little bundles of patches closer to her side, pin her shawl again about her neck, pull her old rag-covered bonnet over her face, and turn her tired feet again to the filling snow path, rather than sit at table or fireside with the pleasantest of hosts," Woolley wrote. "Many a time has my father taken his hat and left the supper table till this weary old creature could eat and go to her slumber; or, if she would journey on, sent his little boy and girl with their aprons full of cookies and doughnuts (from my mother's well-filled table) for the poor wanderer to carry on her way."

In an 1865 letter to an Ohio newspaper that printed Greenwood's story, a former resident of "Upstate New York" stated that she knew Lucy Dutton well, as the strange woman often would walk through her neighborhood in her wanderings and visit her home. "Her appearance was singular in the extreme, as she always so patched her clothes with different colors that the original fabrics could scarcely be distinguished. To cut pieces from her garments, and replace them with any bright bits of cloth she had received, seemed to be her greatest delight, until she more resembled a walking sack for the paper mill, than a human being," according to M. A. Taylor, in her February 15, 1865, letter to the *Jeffersonian Democrat*, in Chardon, Ohio. "In her wanderings, she always carried as many bundles as she could, ornamented with like patches. I have seen her with one bundle under each hand, one under each arm, and one following her on the ground, which was fastened by a string to her waist." Taylor remembered that Lucy would always walk near the fence of any road, so she could easily escape into the adjacent fields to avoid any approaching men.

"She was graceful in her manners, had a low, sweet voice, and always curtsied with much politeness when she entered a dwelling. She was always a welcome visitor, but scarcely ever remained but a short time, if there was a *man* in the family; or, if the children indulged in undue curiosity respecting her appointments, she would gather up her *precious bundles*, and leave," Taylor wrote. "We received only vague reports concerning her last days, but, as the incidents of her life agree perfectly with what was well-known in our vicinity, there is no room to doubt as to the incidents of her death."

An Erieville resident wrote of Lucy in 1885 to an Albany newspaper, verifying the story as told by Grace Greenwood. The writer recalled Lucy as "an object of pity, and was usually treated kindly by those with whom she stopped. Those she would shun she called 'whistling bullies' and would run if one came near her. There are those living here that well remember her as she appeared to them in their youthful days."

In 1885, Henry Severance, who also verified Greenwood's story, recalled of Lucy: "All these long and weary years this woman went her way from house to house, through summer's heat and winter's cold, sleeping at night upon the immense bundle of rags she carried with her, generally taking the more infrequent roads, and always moving slowly under her immense burden of rags. She was feared only for the vermin she might carry with her, an object of pity and compassion, that no rude boy could ever find it in his heart to pester or annoy. She had a soft plaintive voice which she used sparingly, was always fed whenever she desired it, and was never denied food and shelter by anyone."

William W. Crane, who grew up in Nelson during the early nine-teenth century, also remembered Lucy Dutton. "Crazy Lucy used to call, in her endless wanderings, on William's mother, and the impressions made on his infant mind was such that through life he has had very great pity for the insane," Crane wrote in the third person in his 1891 autobi-ography. Crane recalled that Lucy had been jilted on her wedding day, when the bridegroom married her sister, after which Lucy went out and disappeared and could not be found for many days. "It was thought that she was dead, as some of her clothes had been found on the shore of Caze-novia lake," Crane wrote. "When found she was so totally demented that she had no knowledge of passing events, and it seems that she never had one ray of reason until she was dying in the almshouse more than forty years afterwards."

Sutherland and Taylor's writings, as well as the anonymous Erieville resident's letter to the editor, are the only known writings in which some-one who claimed to have known Lucy Dutton commented on and verified the reliability of Grace Greenwood's story. Taylor's writing is also one of the most detailed descriptions of Lucy Dutton as she appeared during her life on record. All these nineteenth century accounts, primary sources or reminiscences from people who knew Lucy, mention her multicolor cloth-ing, her love of carrying in her bundle rags and her bible, and, more than anything, her fear of men. Interestingly, while every story mentions that being jilted on her wedding day was the cause of her insanity, none of the stories relate the actual occurrence other than by hearsay.

Even after the turn of the twentieth century, more than sixty years after Lucy's death, her story still was repeated. Anzolette D. Ellsworth wrote in her 1901 history of New Woodstock and vicinity that "some of the older inhabitants" of New Woodstock still remembered Crazy Luce (who Ellsworth maintained lived in New Woodstock and not in Cazenovia, as Greenwood's story related) and described her as "a person of medium height, possessing some traces of beauty, and having a remarkably sweet voice. Her gown, sometimes ragged, was always patched with many col-ors, and trimmed with balls of yarn. In summer, her bonnet was covered with flowers, which she dearly loved. Her bible, surplus clothing, and bun-dles of rags and herbs were carried on her arm. Harmless in her insanity, at places where she stayed overnight her resting place was preferably the wood house or the cheese room rather than the living rooms if there were men about the house, whom she always avoided if possible."

Dr. F. C. Robinson, who was born and raised in Pompey, about ten miles from Cazenovia, told the *Cazenovia Republican* in 1915 the story of Lucy Dutton, "who occasionally wandered around our neighborhood," as told to him by his mother. In Robinson's story, Lucy's sister, Mary (rather than Ellen), beguiled the bridegroom, whose name was William Maxwell (rather than Edwin W——) and they were married on the day of the previously planned wedding between William and Lucy. When the newlyweds arrived for the wedding, William supposedly explained what had happened, and told Lucy's father, "I did not know what love was until I saw your second daughter. She is my wife. We were married this afternoon while on our way here." Lucy then fell to the floor unconscious.

"The severe shock was followed by brain fever, and when she had recovered from the fever, they found she was insane—her reason entirely dethroned," according to Robinson.

"I remember that sad and sorrowful face, bronzed and wrinkled by the summer's sun and winter's frost—the wild, gleaming eye, restless manner, clad in a dress of many pieces and colors, always trying to avoid meeting men everywhere. Time had left many, many marks upon the brow of Lucy Dutton. She was young and yet she was old," Robinson wrote. "Her sweet voice and song appealed to the heart of a little boy, as I was then, and the story of Lucy Dutton comes back to me as one of childhood's fitful dreams."

A 1931 article in the *Cazenovia Republican* recalled the story of Crazy Luce, particularly as told by Grace Greenwood. According to the article, Greenwood (Mrs. Sarah Jane Lippincott) was born in Pompey in 1823 and died in New Rochelle in 1904. "Everybody read Grace Greenwood's stories once, but that was a long time ago," the article states. After telling the story of Lucy Dutton, the author concluded, "Years ago girls used to read the story of Lucy Dutton and weep, but she is forgotten. Few probably even at New Woodstock remember that 'Crazy Luce' ever lived. Some have heard their fathers tell of her, but not many."

According to a 1947 article by George W. Walter in the *Mid York Weekly*, a man named William Edgarton told about Lucy visiting his grandparents' house, and how his grandmother would invite Lucy to sleep by the fireplace. "Luce would never come in tho, until all the men folks had gone to bed," he said. His grandfather told him how afraid of men Luce was, and that "if she saw a man coming along the road as she was walking along, she would leave the road and go off into the fields to avoid them." According to Walter, Lucy was born in New Hampshire in about 1772, and came with her parents and sister to New Woodstock "with the early pioneers."

One of the most recent articles about Crazy Luce was by June Bergman and published in the *Cazenovia Republican* in June 1971. Bergman relates the generally known story of Lucy Dutton and explores the various discrepancies and similarities in many of the tales through the years. For example, did Lucy live in Cazenovia, New Woodstock, Nelson, or Madison? Was her bridegroom's name Edwin W. or Edwin Morrell? Did she wander around Madison County or Onondaga County? Bergman stated she had searched through old records and explored local cemeteries but never found any tangible evidence of Lucy Dutton's life or death.

However, there has been a new discovery that changes the story of Crazy Luce as has been known, told, and retold in Cazenovia for more than 170 years.

The Original Crazy Luce Story Discovered

Every retelling of Lucy Dutton's story in newspapers and history books after 1847 references Grace Greenwood's story "A Night of Years" as the original tale. But another article has been found dating to eleven years before Greenwood's story was first published, which relates Lucy's life in a much different way, although with many similarities to the better-known tale. A reading of this earlier article makes clear that Grace Greenwood was retelling a previously told story—and that the history of Crazy Luce was much different the first time around.

In the March 15, 1836, issue of the *Cortland Republican* newspaper, page one was taken up entirely by a story titled "Crazy Luce, or a Correct History of the Life and Adventures of the Wandering Woman." This story, which contains no author's byline, relates the pathetic story of sixteen-year-old Lucy Denmore, "a beautiful girl . . . as cheerful as the lark that awoke her with its morning song." Lucy lived with her spinster aunt on the eastern side of a lake (apparently Cazenovia Lake), the opposite side from the "flourishing and delightful village." Both of Lucy's parents were dead, and her only sister, Maria, lived in the west of the state.

The beautiful maiden Lucy was the favorite of the village's young men, all of whom sighed whenever they passed her door and cast a sidelong glance "to catch a glimpse of her fairy form." One day, as she was walking through the woods, picking flowers, she met a man out hunting named Eugene Mervyn, who had only recently moved into the nearby village. They struck up a conversation; he walked her home and told his friend later that he had become instantly beguiled by as beautiful a creature as he had ever seen.

After that, Mervyn's boat could be seen almost daily moored across the lake near the Denmore cottage, where he would spend hours conversing with Lucy and her aunt. Once he won the aunt's favor, he and Lucy were allowed to walk alone together down the lawn. "Here would Mervyn breathe forth his own vows of love, and receive an answer in the averted eye, half hid beneath the long dark eyelashes of the blushing fair one, the gentle heaving of her snowy bosom, and the whispered note of affection; for he had contrived to steal away her heart, with an art to which he was no stranger," according to the story. "The purest feelings of that artless, confiding girl had yielded entirely to the magic of his insinuations, and her whole soul was his."

For Eugene, however, the relationship was merely a flirtation, and once Lucy gave in and admitted she loved him with all her heart, he lost interest, telling his friend he would be humiliated to marry such a poor orphan girl. In order to rid himself of her, Mervyn decided to leave for a village in the west of the state, where he would stay until she should get over her "foolish attachment to him." He told her he would return soon, but he was gone for months and did not contact Lucy at all.

While Lucy nursed her heartbreak, she received a letter from her sister saying she had fallen in love with a man she met out west and was returning as his wife. When the couple reached the Denmore home, her husband was none other than Eugene Mervyn. Lucy was devastated, and her sister had no idea why. She did not know her husband was her sister's lost love. Eugene stood frozen, he "stood like a murderer before the body of his victim," while Lucy went pale and passed out in her sister's arms.

Maria watched by the side of her sister's bed all night, while Lucy made relentless insane rantings and eventually "sank down in a state of childish imbecility." Maria fell asleep, and when she woke Lucy was gone. Maria and Eugene searched all over for Lucy but could not find her. At last, Eugene found Lucy's handkerchief in the woods, near the spot where he first met her, by the lake's edge. It was assumed Lucy drowned, and the shock of that grief quickly killed Maria. Eugene survived, believing himself the murderer of poor Lucy by breaking her heart, and thereby the murderer of his wife who also died of heartache.

Many years after the events of the story, the writer stated, he found himself in Cazenovia, where one of the first things he saw upon entering the village was "a wretched woman, surrounded by a dozen idle urchins, who found her a fit subject for their sport. Her garments were a confused mass of many-colored rags, heaped one upon another, until the wearer was made to appear like a huge walking bundle. From either arm were suspended three or four budgets filled with rags, which the boys were filching from her; and roaring with laughter on witnessing her embarrassment when she missed one of her favorites. Her eyes were constantly fixed upon the ground; a slight grizzly beard covered her chin, and deep furrows were traced in her cheeks, and on her brow."

As the boys continued to torment the poor woman, and one prepared to trip her into the dust, a passerby chastised the boys and told them to "respect the miseries of the unfortunate." The passerby turned out to be Eugene Mervyn's old friend, who said the wretched woman was none other than Lucy Denmore, whom the people now called Crazy Luce. He then told the story of Lucy and Eugene—which was the story as written by the author—and said that Lucy did not drown as everyone believed, but was found some time later, miles away, wandering the road. She refused to return to her home, and remembered no one, not even her aunt. Neighbors would confine her to her aunt's house, but Lucy always escaped and went back to wandering the roads, "begging patches, needles and thread, and busying herself, whenever she rested from the fatigues of her journey, in sewing patch after patch upon her different articles of dress."

At all seasons of the year, in every kind of weather, Crazy Luce would wander the roads. "At sight of a man she always fled, but with those of her own sex she would sometimes converse with all the simplicity of a child," according to the story. "If a worm lay in her path, she would tread aside. Gentleness had ever been her very nature." By the writing of the story in 1836, Lucy was dead, the writer stated. But before she died, her reason was

LEGENDS & LORE
"CRAZY LUCE"
LUCY DUTTON, LIVED CA. 1795
NEAR CAZENOVIA LAKE, JILTED
BY MAN WHO WED HER SISTER,
WENT MAD AND WANDERED
MADISON COUNTY FOR 30 YEARS
NEW YORK FOLKLORE SOCIETY
WILLIAM G. POMEROY FOUNDATION 2015   14

12. The story of Crazy Luce is such a Cazenovia legacy that in 2015 the New York Folklore Society and William G. Pomeroy Foundation erected a New York Historical Marker at the foot of Cazenovia Lake explaining who Lucy was. Photo by Jason Emerson.

"partially restored," although she remembered nothing after the moment Eugene and Maria returned home and announced their marriage all those years before.

Who Was Crazy Luce?

The stories of Crazy Luce as told in 1836 versus 1847 have as many similarities as they do differences—and some of the differences can be found in the reminiscences of people who claimed to have actually seen and known Lucy herself. First and most obvious, the names are different: Lucy Dutton versus Lucy Denmore; Edwin W—— versus Eugene Mervyn. Lucy's family situation is different (her parents alive versus dead, her sister at home or away), how she met her fiancé is different, the culpability of her sister in stealing the bridegroom away is different, as are the fates of the sister and groom after Lucy's breakdown, and whether it was believed Lucy was dead or not immediately after suffering her collapse. (Interestingly, only one story repeats the 1836 statement that Lucy was believed dead after her breakdown, based on one of her belongings being found near the lakeshore—William W. Crane's 1891 autobiography.)

Names and family relationships can be mistaken, forgotten, and misconstrued, while stories can change slightly in each telling, as everyone knows who has ever played the game of "Telephone." The major difference in these two versions of the same story lies in exactly how and by whom Lucy got her heart broken. In the 1836 version, it was the shallow and selfish Eugene who was completely to blame for leading her on then deserting her, only to return married to her unknowing sister. In the 1847 version, Lucy is not deserted but is the one who leaves (stays behind) in order to prepare the wedding; while the villain is Lucy's younger sister, who purposely seduces Edwin to steal him away from Lucy. These differences are too major to be the simple alterations of hearsay. Are they evidence that one, or both, of the stories are fiction? Or do they reflect the social mores of the decades in which they were written, with the authors seeking to conform to the literary norms of the time—blaming the philandering beau versus blaming the "traitoress sister"?

However, there is another interesting difference in the way Lucy is characterized in 1836 versus 1847. In the earlier version—the version closest in time to Lucy's life—she is a pathetic, broken woman, one who goes "begging" for her clothing patches, who converses "with all the simplicity of a child," and gets tormented by local boys in the village. She is "wretched," too pathetic to look anywhere but at the ground, has a "slight grizzled beard" and "deep furrows traced in her cheeks, and on her brow." In short, she is an ugly, pitiful vagrant. But in 1847, Lucy is bright and gay, somewhat tattered, but covered in colorful patches with a bonnet adorned with wildflowers; an easy, spritely woman who often visits with other women in their homes. Yes, she is afraid of men, but she simply exits the roads and walks in the fields to avoid them, as would any person seeking to avoid something or someone unpleasant. In this version, Lucy is odd, somewhat lamentable, but not at all the dirty vagabond she is made to be in 1836.

Why the difference in Lucy's character after only eleven years? All the similarities of the stories of Crazy Luce concern Lucy losing her fiancé to her sister, and what her life was like after that happened, from her wanderings to her patchwork clothing, to her fear of all men, and her final lucidity in the moments before she died. The fact that every story sticks to this script, as do all the reminiscences by people who claimed to have seen and known Lucy personally, makes it as certain as possible that Crazy Luce was indeed a real person who wandered the roads of Cazenovia and Madison County, a woman whom her neighbors would take in and show compassion and charity. And yet, despite the overwhelming evidence that Lucy Dutton was a real person who was seen, known, and remembered by many of her neighbors, no documentary proof has yet been found to verify who she was, who her family members were or where they lived, or who her fiancé was and where he lived. This is not surprising given the early date of these occurrences, the lack of written records from the early 19th century and the ease of their accidental destruction (usually through structure fires), but it is still troubling.

In the end, is the story of Crazy Luce as told by Grace Greenwood—the version that has lived and thrived since 1847—the true account of Lucy Dutton/Denmore, or is the more pathetic vagrant of 1836, tricked and tossed aside by a cruel young man, more akin to the authentic person that has become a long-told folk tale? Or is she simply a fiction created by an enterprising writer?

Whether Crazy Luce lived in Cazenovia or New Woodstock, whether she was tricked by her beau or betrayed by her sister, whether she was dirty and pitiable or colorful and innocent, her story of heartbreak and itinerancy has become one of Cazenovia's most famous local legends. As June Bergman wrote in 1971, "Legend or fact, let no family claim her as their own. She belongs to all of us. Her memory to be cherished and treasured as one would treasure a family heirloom."

The Mother of American Kindergarten
Susan Blow and Her Time in Cazenovia

From kindergarten through high school graduation, Cazenovia students enjoy an excellent public education, for which the town is rightly proud. Considerable thanks for that education lies with a former resident of the village, Susan Blow, known as the Mother of American Kindergarten. Blow, who began the early childhood education movement in America, spent her retirement years in Cazenovia in a home on Sullivan Street. She took an active role in education both nationally and here in Cazenovia and Cazenovians have her to thank for the early childhood education system their children enjoy today.

Born in St. Louis in 1843 to a wealthy family, Susan Blow received a private education both in Missouri and New Orleans, a rare benefit for a woman at the time. Her parents, Henry and Minerva Blow, held progressive ideas and felt that a strong education was the best foundation for all of their children. Henry had also formed strong abolitionist sentiments during his childhood, which he would pass on to Susan and her siblings. Henry's parents had owned slaves, one in particular being Dred Scott, famous for the 1857 Supreme Court case bearing his name. Henry and his brother Taylor donated legal aid and funds to support their former slave in his suit for freedom against his new owner and, although Scott lost, the Blows would later help him obtain his freedom.

Henry, a successful iron and lead mining industrialist, entered politics when Susan was eleven. He served a term in the Missouri senate before being appointed by President Abraham Lincoln as the Minister to Venezuela. He returned to the United States shortly after the outbreak of the Civil War and was elected to the House of Representatives in 1862,

13. Susan Blow, founder of the American early education movement. Courtesy of the State Historical Society of Missouri.

where he helped fight for the abolitionist agenda. He and Susan's mother developed a friendship with the Lincolns during their time in Washington which would last until Mary Lincoln's death in 1882. President Ulysses S. Grant appointed Henry minister to Brazil in 1869. Susan and her family accompanied him, with Susan acting as her father's secretary.

Shortly after, Susan traveled to Europe where she studied the educational teachings of Friedrich Froebel, a leader in early childhood education. Blow was deeply attracted to Froebel's theories on childhood development and the connection between play and cognitive growth. When she returned to the United States, she received educator training at the New York Normal Training Kindergarten School and in 1873 opened the nation's first public kindergarten in Carondelet, Missouri, at the Des Peres School. The experiment was so successful that within three years the kindergartens in the area had expanded to enroll over one thousand children.

The program, based around Froebel's educational philosophy, emphasized the use of song, manipulatives, and hands-on experimentation to teach students numbers, letters, responsibility, and independence. Blow was certain that providing children with a bright, colorful room full of plants, music, and furniture just their size would encourage them to put their natural inquiry skills to use. She and her patron, St. Louis School Superintendent William Torrey Harris, argued that providing a strong educational foundation early on would decrease the alarming dropout rate facing older students. Many of Blow's original ideas, such as the connection between physical play and cognitive development, comprise the bedrock of early childhood education today.

As Susan Blow's kindergarten gained popularity in Missouri, she set up teacher training schools and kindergarten systems across the region, and eventually across the country. In 1884, she retired from teaching due to Graves' disease (an immune system disorder that results in hyperthyroidism) but she didn't slow down. She moved to Boston and went on to help found the International Kindergarten Union, and was appointed to the Teachers College of Columbia University. Many of her writings at this time, including "Symbolic Education" and "The Songs and Music of Froebel's Mother Play," are considered seminal works in early childhood education.

In 1895, Blow purchased a summer home in Cazenovia at 8 Sullivan Street. The address is currently occupied by the Cazenovia College Shove Hall, though whether the Susan Blow House, as it came to be known, was moved or demolished is unknown. She would use the Cazenovia home, which she usually shared with her niece, Miss Nelka deSmirnoff, or her private secretary, as the base from which she traveled extensively on lecture tours of the northeast and Midwest. Blow was extremely well known by the 1890s and her arrival generated much excitement in the village.

The *Cazenovia Republican* edition of February 1895 enthusiastically proclaimed: "After denying rumors to the contrary for a number of months, we are able this week to authoritatively announce that B. Vollmer has sold his residence on Sullivan Street to Miss S. Blow." She was known to spend every summer among the villagers from 1895 until her death in New York City in 1916.

Cazenovia had opened its own kindergarten classroom in 1891 under the tutelage of Miss Vinnie Atwell, who was a devotee of Blow's program. She, too, had studied Froebel's principles and had trained at a kindergarten in Syracuse. The Cazenovia school was located over the Watkins Bookstore on Lincklaen Street and enrolled nearly twenty village children in its first year. Tuition was five dollars per term and classes ran from 9 a.m. to noon. As set out in Blow's system, Atwell's school emphasized physical activity, singing, and hands-on play. "A thousand and one things are learned which lay the foundation for a future education," according to a newspaper article from 1891. Atwell designed the room to be colorful and varied the lessons from day to day, including different songs and stories with each day's object lesson. This system, instituted by Blow, differed significantly from traditional classrooms of the day, where students sat at benches or desks for long periods, memorizing facts and reciting rote material.

Atwell worked closely with Susan Blow during her years in the village, cohosting a Kindergarten Conference in Cazenovia with her in August 1896. Atwell had charge of the visitors, "in a way that left little or nothing to be desired," according to one attendee. During the two-week conference, Blow delivered a series of lectures to over eighty "kindergartners," as professionals in the system were known, representing nearly every state as well as from as far away as Japan. It was the largest gathering of kindergarten educators ever convened at the time and it speaks to the momentum around the movement. Blow was joined at the convention by Dr. Smith Baker, a leading psychologist, and Dr. William Torrey Harris, United States Commissioner of Education, all advocating for the Froebel method of early childhood education. Blow's lectures were centered around the subjects of "The Kindergarten Gifts" and "Mother Play" as well as on detailed instruction of educational games and exercises.

The Presbyterian church played host to the conference, while many in the village generously opened their homes to the visiting educators "and

14. A typical Froebel-style kindergarten room. Note the animal silhouettes on the wall, the manipulatives on the table, and the low benches, all hallmarks of a twenty-first century kindergarten classroom. Courtesy of the State Historical Society of Missouri.

extended numerous courtesies, which were fully appreciated by every member of the conference," according to Henry Blake, one of the attendees. Blake recalled that evenings were dedicated to kindergarten games; "the games occurred in the old rink or 'Harlem Opera House,'" he said, "and at times there were sixty skilled kindergartners in the circle." The conference was not all "sober business," according to Blake, since "[time] was divided between driving, rowing and sailing on the lake, and patronizing the local bicycle liveries," he said. The conference of 1896 was considered an unqualified success for the kindergartners and would help to add fuel to the movement sweeping the nation.

For Susan Blow though, Cazenovia was more than just a charming summer retreat. She took a personal interest in the education of village children. In 1901, she turned her attention to the youth of Cazenovia, specifically the young men. She proposed an evening program in the basement of the Union schoolhouse, dedicated to physical arts. In a letter to the newspaper in 1901, she argued that the young ladies of the village were taught cooking and sewing to refine their practical skills, but that the young men were left with only idle pursuits. Blow planned a program based around military drills, gymnastic exercises, and a Swedish-based woodworking craft known as sloyd. The program had the support of many civic-minded citizens, including the local clergy, the school principal, and notable personages such as the Krumbhaars and Burrs. It became known as the Boys' Club and was a rapid success and "productive of so much good last winter," according to a 1902 *Cazenovia Republican* article. To support the organization, Blow gave literature lectures; "a rare treat," said the newspaper, "for Miss Blow is herself a writer of national repute and abundantly prepared to give a most interesting address."

Despite her ill health, Blow traveled constantly, sharing her theories on childhood development and the importance of education with teachers and administrators around the country. She remained on the lecture circuit until a month before her death in 1916 at the age of seventy-three. At the time of her death, she was making plans to return to her beloved summer home in Cazenovia and had contacted her gardener John Dean to prepare the home for her arrival. Though she was buried in St. Louis, her Cazenovia friends would not soon forget her and all that she contributed to the village. For many years her name was mentioned in the newspaper as her relatives, the deSmirnoffs and Moukanhoffs, continued to visit the area. And the Boys' Club that she helped found would continue to enrich the lives of young men for years to come. Her most important contribution to Cazenovia society, however, would be the strength of the village kindergarten, based on her model and incorporated into the Cazenovia Central School system by the middle of the twentieth century. The village was made richer not just by her acclaim but by her influence on the exceptional education Cazenovian children enjoy nearly 150 years later.

William J. Hough Helped Create the Smithsonian Institution

If a person's impact on the world is gauged by the number of lives they touch, then William J. Hough's influence on posterity is legendary. Although he was a resident of Cazenovia for more than twenty-five years and an influential citizen, soldier, and politician, it is the fact that he authored the final legislation to create the Smithsonian Institution—what has become the largest museum and research organization in the world—and was one of the institution's first regents that has become Hough's claim to fame.

William Jarvis Hough was born in the Oneida County town of Paris Hill in 1795. His family moved to Pompey Hill in Onondaga County when he was a child and he attended school at the Pompey Hill Academy. He studied law and clerked in the office of Childs & Stebbins in Cazenovia and was admitted to the bar in 1820. Hough married Clarinda Carpenter in Cazenovia in 1821. They moved to Lyons, Ontario (now Wayne County), New York, where Hough opened a law office. In 1828, the couple moved back to Cazenovia, where they lived until 1855.

In Cazenovia, the Houghs raised their three children in a stately home on the south side of the public square, still known as "Hough House." Hough was a prominent citizen of Cazenovia during his time there. He was an attorney as well as a businessman, and owned a general store in the Rouse Building called "The Regulator" in which was sold dress material, china, carpets, hardware, and groceries. He was also a prominent general in the state militia and was tendered a brigadier generalship during the Mexican War by President James K. Polk, although Hough never served on active duty in Mexico. Because of his military service (which started long before the Mexican War), Hough was known as "General

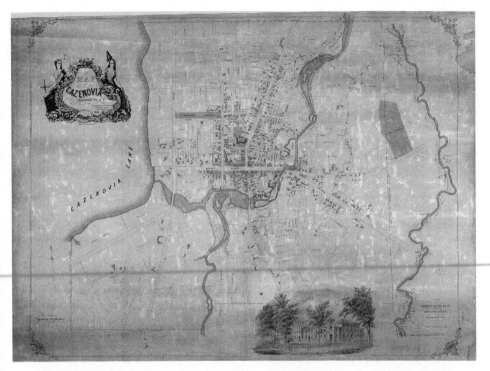

15. Map of Cazenovia from 1852. Included in the village map is the location of the Hough family home on the south side of the public square on Albany Street, as well as the building Hough owned at the corner of Albany and Lincklaen streets in which he housed his general store, called "The Regulator." Courtesy of the Library of Congress.

Hough" throughout most of his adult life. He was also a trustee of Cazenovia Seminary.

Hough was also extremely active in local, state, and national politics. In Cazenovia, he served as president of the village twice (1838 and 1841) and as clerk of the village twice (1829 and 1833). In newspaper archives he is frequently listed as a member of various community organizations and committees, such as those preparing for community celebrations or undertaking municipal improvements. In 1835 and 1836, Hough served as a member of the New York State Assembly, representing Madison and Chenango Counties. In 1844, Hough was elected as a Democrat to the Twenty-Ninth US Congress (March 5, 1845, to March 3, 1847), representing

16. Painting of William Hough and family. Courtesy of the National Portrait Gallery, Smithsonian Institution, Washington, DC; gift of Violet Shepherd.

the Twenty-Third District of New York. The major work of that Congress included admitting Texas as a state and declaring war against Mexico after a military clash in the disputed Texas territory. The Congress also admitted Iowa to the union and the House passed the Postage Stamp Act—authorizing the use of postage stamps in the United States for the first time.

Hough's Congressional tenure is best remembered, however, for his role in the creation of the Smithsonian Institution. He was the congressman who authored the final draft of the bill establishing the institution in 1846. The bill introduced the term "regent" in relation to the governing of the Smithsonian and set aside the land (west of Seventh Street to the Potomac River) on which to build the new museum. According to the official history of the Smithsonian, Hough served on the Board of Regents and at its first meeting on September 9, 1846, was elected interim secretary to lead the institution until the permanent secretary, Joseph Henry, was named in December of that year. Hough also served on the committee that directed the construction of the Smithsonian Castle and was "a leading force in the shaping of the fledgling institution." Hough's portrait and a portrait of his family are still displayed in the Castle East Wing, along with other regents.

Hough returned from Congress in 1847 and continued to live in Cazenovia until about 1855, when he moved to Syracuse. There, he created a new law practice, served as the vice president for the Syracuse City Bank, and was president of the city's Board of Education for two terms. He died in Syracuse on October 4, 1869. "He was a successful business man, and in all public and private relations enjoyed the highest respect and confidence of all who knew him," said his obituary in the *Syracuse Journal*. Hough is buried in Oakwood Cemetery, Syracuse.

Elizabeth Smith Miller,
the Original Bloomer

Much has been written about the remarkable life and times of Elizabeth Smith Miller: activist, reformer, and philanthropist. She is known for her work in the woman's rights movement as well as for her illustrious salons featuring the best and brightest of the nation's thinkers. But it may be her revolutionary take on women's clothing shortly after moving from Cazenovia for which she is best remembered.

Elizabeth was the only daughter—and some claim favored child—of congressman and abolitionist Gerrit Smith. She was born in Peterboro, New York, in 1822 and enjoyed a liberal upbringing on her family's palatial estate. At her father's knee she absorbed progressive ideas about basic human equality regardless of race or sex. In her adult life, these same ideas would launch her into the forefront of woman's rights organizations.

In 1843 Elizabeth married Charles Dudley Miller, a cashier at the Madison County Bank at Cazenovia. He would later serve an appointment as colonel during the Civil War. Miller seems to have wholly approved of Elizabeth's progressive ideas and supported her choices throughout their marriage. He not only joined her in signing petitions and participating in woman's rights conventions, but he also generously funded the movement throughout his life. The couple married in Peterboro and chose to make their home in Cazenovia where Charles was employed. For three years they called the house at 15 Sullivan Street home. The current structure has since been modified many times and it is unclear if this is the same building that stood at the spot at the time of the Millers' residence. In 1846, they decamped for a luxurious cottage on her parents' estate in Peterboro and later to Lochland, an estate in Geneva, New York.

THE BLOOMER COSTUME.

17. A mid-nineteenth-century example of the Bloomer costume as may have been worn by Elizabeth Smith Miller. Courtesy of the Library of Congress.

It was shortly after their time in Cazenovia that Elizabeth made a decision that would echo down the centuries. Around 1850, she modified her long skirts to make gardening easier, shortening the skirt and adding loose pants underneath. "I became so thoroughly disgusted with the long skirt, that the dissatisfaction . . . suddenly ripened into the decision that this shackle should no longer be endured. The resolution was at once put into practice. Turkish trousers to the ankle with a skirt reaching some four inches below the knee, were substituted for the heavy, untidy, and exasperating old garment," she later said.

She continued to wear the costume around town, where it started a remarkable trend among the ladies of Madison County. The *Madison County Whig* reported in 1851 that "Mrs. Miller has already made her new substitute very popular in Peterboro, where it is worn so commonly as to have ceased to attract attention." She eventually wore it on a trip to Seneca Falls to visit her cousin Elizabeth Cady Stanton. During the visit, both Stanton and her friend Amelia Bloomer were so enamored of this revolution in dress that they adopted the costume themselves and began promoting it through their publications. "Many of the women of her village [of Seneca Falls] have already adopted the dress, and in the costume reform, thus auspiciously began, the unmentionables are steadily displacing the no-you-don't-ables," the *Madison County Whig* reported.

Amelia Bloomer espoused the many benefits of the less restrictive costume in her temperance magazine *Lily* and it came to be known as the "Bloomer Costume" thereafter. According to Bloomer, "At the outset, I had no idea of fully adopting the style; no thought of setting a fashion; no thought that my action would create an excitement throughout the civilized world and give to the style my name and the credit due Mrs. Miller." Newspapers throughout Central New York who knew Elizabeth Smith Miller to be the inventor called for a name change to the Miller Costume, though the admittedly more vivid name, Bloomer, was already connected with the outfit and would remain so indefinitely.

The fashion was quickly adopted by many in the feminist movement as a symbol of their rejection of patriarchal confinement. Reactions from the public ranged from amusement to scandalized horror. "We are at last enabled to answer a question propounded by our correspondents," sneers a brevity in the *Madison County Whig*. "'What is a Bloomer?' 'One who *pants* for notoriety.'" A journalist reporting on a woman's rights convention in

New York City wrote derisively, "The Bloomer toilets I saw on that eventful day will never be forgotten by me, if I should live for a hundred years."

The distinctive look faded from popularity among many early adopters by the 1870s. It may have been that the leadership in the movement was striving for professionalism above practicality at this time and the costume was becoming a distraction. Elizabeth Miller, however, would continue to wear the revolutionary outfit "with the full sanction and approval of her father and husband," according to Bloomer. She even appeared in the costume in Washington, DC, where she hosted parties for her father during his tenure in congress.

The Cazenovian reaction to Elizabeth's invention was mixed. Many editorials in the local newspapers expressed outrage. Antifeminist contributor Thomas Snarlyle decried it in the *Cazenovia Gazette* as "A sort of shemale dress you call Bloomerism." Others seemed to celebrate their trailblazing hometown heroine and followed the progress of the fashion across the Atlantic. "The Bloomer Costume has been adopted by several young ladies at Harrogate, a fashionable English watering place," the *Madison County Journal* reported in 1851. The *Madison County Whig* took a humorous point of view: "The 'Bloomers' of Ellicottville were out on horseback on the Fourth, to the number of six or seven, and—rode-astride!—The words of an honest man for that, who was there and saw them. But don't faint yet—it was suspected they were all boys."

Cazenovia became a leader in the woman's rights campaign as it had with other liberal movements such as abolition and temperance. Although Elizabeth had only resided in Cazenovia for three years, she was enthusiastically claimed by the local feminists, among whom she had many friends. By 1865, the *Cazenovia Republican* newspaper was prepared to claim both Mrs. Miller and her invention: "She first wore the costume, since known as the 'Bloomer,' while cultivating her flowers, simply, as we have the best authority of saying, as a matter of convenience and not taste." "The meed of merit," the newspaper asserted, "has not been bestowed where it is deserved." Elizabeth and Charles would continue to support the movement for the next fifty years, serving as delegates, securing funding, and lending their influence to conventions and assemblies.

Elizabeth passed away in May 1911, by this time a well-known supporter of the women's suffrage movement. But after more than fifty years she was still linked to her one-time provocative costume and was

18. Elizabeth Smith Miller, at right, pictured toward the end of her life with Anne Fitzhugh Miller at the Ontario County Woman Suffrage Association Convention in 1909. Courtesy of the Library of Congress.

eulogized as Cazenovia's "Bloomer Girl" by the *Cazenovia Republican* newspaper. "The lady in question will be remembered by all the older residents of Cazenovia. She sang in the Free Church where her father, the late Gerrit Smith, often preached," the newspaper wrote. Her ideas on dress reform and the bloomer costume may have been a passing fad, but the spark she struck within the feminist community continues to this day, living on through advocates for women's health and well-being.

Escape from Confederate Prison

The Civil War Story of William Madge

Everyone loves a good Civil War story. There is just something about that moment in US history that continues to fascinate and captivate Americans even 150 years later. Cazenovian William Madge, who was a prisoner at the infamous Andersonville Confederate prison in 1864, has one of the more exciting tales in his town to come out of the war—a tale of battles, capture, imprisonment, and daring escape; a tale that was so interesting that it was submitted to a national newspaper contest for the best true stories of the war and, while it did not win, was included in a book of stories selected from the contest submissions.

Madge was a twenty-year-old farmhand in Cazenovia when he enlisted in the Union army in July 1861, only three months after the war began when the Confederates attacked Fort Sumter in South Carolina. He signed on for three years of service as a private and was assigned to Company B of the Third NY Cavalry. The regiment fought all over Virginia, serving in the Army of the Potomac and the Army of the James, during which they destroyed southern rail lines, cut telegraph wires, scouted enemy positions, and fought in skirmishes and battles. Madge reenlisted as a veteran volunteer in the Fourth Provisional Cavalry in January 1864 at Pungo, Virginia. It was during his second tour of duty that his story really began.

Madge's regiment was part of a large cavalry force under generals James H. Wilson and August V. Kautz during the Petersburg campaign in June 1864. From June 20 to 28, the Union troops—numbering 5,500 horsemen and sixteen cannon—covered some 350 miles, working to destroy the three railroads that fed Richmond and Petersburg from the south and west and thereby cut Confederate supply lines. The Yankees were stopped on June 25 at the Staunton River Bridge, after which they moved to return to their own lines. Four days later, on June 29, they were intercepted and engaged by Confederate cavalry under generals Wade Hampton and Fitzhugh Lee and several infantry and artillery brigades at what is now known as the First Battle of Reams Station. The Union troops were surrounded and ultimately routed, and the Wilson-Kautz Raid (as it is now known) ended with 1,400 casualties (killed, wounded, captured, or missing) and the loss of all the artillery and wagons.

Madge was one of the many casualties of the raid and was captured along with what he claimed were about one thousand other Yankee soldiers at Reams Station. He ultimately wrote out three versions of his story—two of which were published in the *Cazenovia Republican* newspaper, and one that was published in the *New York Weekly Tribune* and ultimately in a book by the *Tribune* titled *The Three Bummers and Other Stories of the War Told by Soldiers and Sailors*. Here is what happened according to Madge's own words.

The clear, quiet morning of June 29 at Reams Station suddenly broke into the cacophony of "the thunder of artillery, the crash of musketry, and the distant roar of swiftly advancing cavalry." After being surrounded and cut off by the Confederate troops, the Union cavalry forces, "broken and disorganized," fled. Madge watched as his lines broke, and suddenly an artillery shell struck a tree only a few feet in front of him, which nearly knocked him out of his saddle. He spurred his horse to a run with the other members of Company B as the Confederates swarmed over the Union batteries. Madge rode through the throng of fleeing blue-clad soldiers and, reaching an intersection, stopped his horse to ask which way to go. While talking, a sharpshooter's bullet grazed his cheek and struck a nearby tree. He took off down the left-hand road and rode directly into oncoming Confederate troops, after which he was captured "with a dozen revolvers in close proximity to my head."

The prisoners were taken to Stony Creek Station, some twenty-eight miles away, where they were quickly stripped of anything valuable. "I was robbed of everything when I was taken except the clothes I wore and my gold ring, which I was obliged to sell in prison," Madge wrote. The Yankee prisoners were later put on freight cars that ultimately took them to Andersonville prison in Georgia.

Andersonville was built in early 1864 and held more prisoners at any given time than any of the other Confederate military prisons. The prison pen of over 250 acres was surrounded by a stockade of hewed pine logs that varied in height from fifteen to seventeen feet. Sentry boxes stood at ninety-foot intervals along the top of the stockade. Inside, about nineteen feet from the wall, was the "deadline," marked by a simple post and rail fence, which prisoners were forbidden to cross. Guards had orders to shoot any prisoner who crossed the fence, or even reached over it. A branch of Sweetwater Creek, called Stockade Branch, flowed through the prison yard and was the only source of water for most of the prison.

As Madge later wrote: "Here we were turned into a stockade prison and left to amuse ourselves in the best possible way. Prisoners from Danville, Richmond, and Lynchburg were constantly arriving, with others from Grant and Sherman, weekly augmenting our numbers, and making our condition still worse. During the month of August there were 32,000 prisoners in Andersonville [in an area meant to house 10,000], and their condition was truly horrible. Thousands of them were without shelter from the burning sun, heavy dews, and rain storms, which sometimes were of long duration. Hundreds, sick and unable to help themselves, were lying on the wet ground because the hospitals outside were full." Prisoners slept on the bare ground and were fed scanty rations of "coarse meal, dirty beans, and rotten bacon." The number of deaths daily ranged from thirty to one hundred.

As Union troops advanced through the South, Yankee prisoners of war were constantly moved to prevent rescue. Madge was part of a group of prisoners transferred to Camp Lawton in Millen, Georgia, in September. After a brief stay there, he was transferred to other prisons in Savannah, Blackshear Station, and Thomasville. It was on the way to Thomasville that Madge and his friend Bibby decided they had had enough of prison life and would escape or die trying. On the night of December 11, as they sat on the edge of a railroad flatcar, the train stopped on the border of the Okefenokee Swamp to switch tracks. Madge and Bibby saw their chance and slipped off into the darkness without being noticed by the guards.

The pair were on the run through the swamp for the next twenty-seven days. "Desperately cold and hungry," they moved during the night and hid and slept during daytime. They headed south towards the Gulf, and within a few days had crossed from Georgia into Florida. When they came upon plantations, they would head for the slave cabins to ask for food, which was always freely given, along with directions and advice on the best ways to travel to avoid Confederate pickets.

At one mansion, they asked for help from "a large negro who was chopping wood," who eyed them suspiciously and answered their questions with a surly attitude. The duo was wary, but so hungry they headed for the slave quarters anyway and were soon found by the mistress of the plantation carrying a revolver. After they assured her they were not trying to steal her slaves but were simply escaped prisoners looking for food, she invited them into the main house where she fed them and asked numerous questions about the war and the advance of General William T. Sherman's troops and if her plantation was in danger. She was cordial, yet constantly saying that she should have the men retaken but would abide by her word that she would not. And yet Madge was getting suspicious because every time they made as if to leave, she insisted they stay. Finally, they firmly yet hurriedly left the plantation.

In addition to hunger and exhaustion, the fear of capture was a constant companion. Twice they encountered white Southerners, one a man in a Confederate captain's uniform and one a woman, and both times Madge and Bibby got past them by claiming to be soldiers in the forty-fifth Georgia regiment headed home from the front lines. The rebel captain not only believed them but even ferried them across a river that the pair otherwise would have been unable to cross.

On January 6, Madge and his companion reached Clay Landing on the Luwanee river. After lying in a swamp on the river bank all day, in the evening they took a large yawl near the landing and rowed down the river. They fought through high winds, heavy waves, and driving rain, but eventually made it to the Gulf of Mexico "with Cedar Keys and our blockading squadron in full view." The pair continued rowing, raised an old blanket for a sail and, the winds being favorable, reached Cedar Keys early in the afternoon. "When you see your country's flag daily, and are always under its protecting folds, you seldom appreciate its full value, but to us, after long months of imprisonment and twenty-seven days in the Okefenokee, the stripes and stars seemed the living emblem of glory and hope," Madge wrote. "On our journey the slaves were our friends, and we never called upon them for aid in vain, and it would have been next to impossible to have succeeded without their help."

Madge and Bibby spent a week in Cedar Keys before getting transportation to Key West and from there up to New York. Madge wrote to his parents—who had not heard from him for over a year and had no idea whether he was alive or dead—on March 3, 1865, telling them he was alive and back on Union soil. "I have suffered much, more than you can imagine in those Southern hells, where the thousands died and I never expected to see home and its loved ones again; but I could not give up all hope, though I had some hours of despondency. Those were long days last fall as day after day in the beautiful autumn weather, I sat and thought how I could enjoy it if I was where the old flag floated. This is all over now and I have great reason to be thankful that I escaped with my life from rebel hands. I shall have a long story to tell you of my adventures in Dixie when I come home."

Madge returned to Cazenovia about three weeks later for a short furlough. In late May, he returned to his company in Virginia, and was mustered out of service in September at City Point, Virginia, after which he apparently returned home. In March 1866, his family moved to Irving, Iowa, after buying a farm there, but William's father, John, was reportedly disappointed in the property. John traveled back to Cazenovia in October 1866 and, while in town visiting his nephew, he committed suicide by cutting his own throat and stabbing himself in six different places with a jackknife. The neck wound totally severed his windpipe, and yet he lived for fifteen hours after the deed. He could not speak but could communicate in writing, and he apologized for what he did, claiming he was insane at the time.

US census records show that after his father's death, William Madge stayed out west. In 1870 he was living in Boise, Idaho Territory, working as a farmhand, and in the 1880s he was living in Milton, Oregon. It was at this time, in late 1885, that the New York *Tribune* announced it was seeking stories about personal experiences in the Civil War from regular soldiers and sailors—not from generals or admirals. These "new stories of the war" were solicited with the promise that the best of all submissions would receive a $250 prize, and the runner-up would receive $100. The *Tribune* received over five hundred submissions from across the country and even across the world. Of those, the editors—specifically the prize editor Edmund C. Stedman—chose twenty-seven of the best to be printed in the newspaper, and two of those twenty-seven to win the award.

William B. Madge, living in Oregon, decided to compose a full version of his personal story of escape from Confederate imprisonment, and submitted it to the *Tribune* contest as "Twenty-Seven Days in the Okefenokee Wilderness." His story was chosen as one of the twenty-seven best and published in the *Tribune*'s 1887 book, *The Three Bummers and Other Stories of the War Told by Soldiers and Sailors*.

By 1890, Madge was living in Weston, Oregon, and in 1900, at age sixty, he was in Los Angeles, living in the National Home for Disabled Volunteer Soldiers. Madge died tragically in 1908, when his home caught fire and he burned to death. According to the news report, "Billy" Madge was on a furlough from the Soldiers' Home living in a small cottage he built for himself some years previously in Santa Monica, California. He lived alone and was "almost helpless from rheumatism." Every night he took morphine to help him sleep. His friend and neighbor told the newspaper that he stopped in that night to give Madge his morphine, left him sleeping in his invalid's chair (he no longer used his bed), and left a lamp burning. Neighbors later heard a small explosion, which was assumed by authorities to be the lamp exploding. Madge, being an invalid, could neither escape the house nor call for help, and his body was found "burned to a cinder" amid the house ruins.

The *Los Angeles Herald* reported that not much was known of Madge's personal life, other than that he was a native of Cazenovia, New York, and had fought in the Civil War in the Third NY Cavalry, and "it is said that one time he was prominent as an instructor and also as a historian." He was related to the Roosevelt family by marriage, through his cousin Mrs. Alice Roosevelt, of Cazenovia. Madge's remains were interred with military honors in the cemetery of the National Soldiers' Home in Sawtelle, California.

The Men behind the Famous Cazenovia GAR Photograph

In 2007, the popular public television show *History Detectives* delved into a mystery involving a rare photograph of an integrated group of Civil War veterans from Central New York. The photograph of members of a Grand Army of the Republic (GAR) post was originally discovered by antiquarian Lynda Copper at a 2004 estate sale at a home on the corner of Liberty and Union Streets, in Cazenovia. "I saw this photo and just wanted it," Copper said. The photograph, which dates from around 1900, had lain among a hodgepodge of photos and documents accumulated over three or four generations of the home's owners. "I bought it because I thought it was important," she said. "Any early photograph of Afro-Americans, I buy." And she was not alone in her hunch about the photo's value.

Within two years, the photograph had made its way to collector Angelo Scarlato, who approached the *History Detectives* seeking the provenance of the unusual photo that featured two African American veterans among an otherwise white group. The program's researchers worked to identify the two men and explain their presence in a photo at a time when racial integration was virtually unheard of. The two were identified as Alberta Robbins and John Stevenson, veterans of the Civil War who settled in the Cazenovia area. According to Cazenovia historian Sue Greenhagen, the tiny village had only about forty Black residents at the time of the conflict. Many Union states, including New York, were not particularly welcoming to African Americans serving in the Army, so the presence of the two veterans in this setting is striking.

The *History Detectives* focused on identifying the men and on the significance of Cazenovia's veteran association, the GAR Knowlton Post

19. The GAR Knowlton Post Number 160 Memorial Day photo circa 1900. The photo was unearthed in Cazenovia and featured on the PBS *History Detectives* program in 2007. Public domain image.

Number 160, and its role in forming bonds between soldiers of disparate backgrounds. "If you'd suffered, if you'd sacrificed, you were a comrade. Comradeship explained the interracial GAR," said historian Barbara Gannon of the African American Civil War Museum on the program. Through their research, the show's historians were even able to locate John Stevenson's great-grandson, George Geder, and share his ancestor's story with him.

The photograph has become a famous symbol of Cazenovia's inclusive past, but what about Alberta Robbins and John Stevenson themselves? What were their roles, not only in the war, but in their home community? And what kind of world did these men return to after risking their lives to preserve their country?

Alberta Robbins, the man standing in the rear of the photo, significantly seen holding the flag, was born in Peterboro, New York, in 1840. For the majority of his life he would work in various positions, notably as coachman, for the family of Gerrit Smith Miller, grandson of the legendary abolitionist Gerrit Smith. At the time of his wife Sarah's 102nd birthday in 1945, she was known as the oldest person in Cazenovia and the last to have known Gerrit Smith personally.

Living in close proximity to the nation's leading abolitionist must have had a profound effect on Alberta. He would have had a front row seat to Smith's teachings on racial equality and his outspoken support for the enlistment of African Americans into the Army. Perhaps with those opinions in mind, Alberta chose to enlist in the 55th Massachusetts Infantry Regiment. The 55th was created in 1863 to accept the overabundance of recruits from the 54th Massachusetts Infantry Regiment, the first Black military unit in the United States. The 55th were based mainly out of South Carolina and saw numerous battles throughout the South, including at James Island, Honey Hill, and Briggen Creek. They also marched into conquered Charleston in 1865 to the cheers of former slaves. The 55th faced incredible challenges during the war, frequently tasked with scouting for other regiments or digging trenches while under fire from Confederate troops. As if these tasks were not risky enough, Alberta Robbins performed them without a weapon. Robbins bore the honorable, but dangerous, role of color-bearer for his unit. His role would have been as a visual landmark for the soldiers as well as a motivating symbol to continue into the face of danger. Considering the frequency with which flag-bearers were wounded, it is perhaps astonishing that Alberta escaped harm to be mustered out of service with his compatriots of the 55th in September 1865.

Alberta returned to Smithfield, near Peterboro, where he married Sarah Van Horne, granddaughter of escaped slaves who had found refuge on Gerrit Smith's expansive settlement. The two continued to work for the Smith-Miller household, during which time Alberta was active in the local Temperance movement in the 1870s and held a position of respect as coachman for the well-known family. In the late 1880s, when they moved their family to Cazenovia, Alberta and Sarah had four children—Charles, George, Frankie, and Gertie; a fifth, Sarah, would be born soon after. Alberta took up work as a laborer and teamster in Cazenovia, perhaps the best work he could find without the ability to read and write. The *Cazenovia Republican* newspaper said Alberta was "a faithful worker and performed his duties in such a manner that he never lacked employment." He continued to maintain an excellent reputation throughout the village, despite his son Charles's occasional run-ins with the police.

In 1902, at the installation of the GAR Knowlton Post 160 in Cazenovia, Alberta was elected color-bearer, a position of honor within an organization that claimed many prominent citizens. The famous photo of the GAR group was taken towards the end of Alberta's life. He would pass away a short time later after a bout of pneumonia in 1907, at age sixty-seven. His obituary called him "one of Cazenovia's most respected colored citizens." The GAR performed his burial services at Evergreen Cemetery, confirming their respect for a fellow veteran and honored citizen, regardless of the color of his skin.

Only a short distance away from Alberta's final resting place in Evergreen Cemetery lies John Stevenson, the second African American featured in the photo, seen seated in the middle right of the group. We know less about John's early life compared to his comrade Alberta, except what can be gleaned from census records. He was born in Maryland, possibly in Parma, in 1832 and relocated to the Cazenovia area in the decade before the Civil War.

John, too, chose to enlist in the Army and defend his country. He joined the famed 29th Regiment Connecticut Volunteers when it was established in 1863 and participated in numerous conflicts from their position in Virginia. The 29th would engage the Confederate Army in several skirmishes including the Battle of Kell House, Chaffin's Farm, and the final battle before taking Richmond. Early in 1865, the regiment was shipped to Texas before finally returning home toward the end of the year.

John returned to Cazenovia shortly after the war to resume his job as farmer and laborer. He and his wife Martha are listed in census records as unable to read or write, but it certainly did not stop them from enjoying a full life on the merits of their hard work. Unlike many wage laborers of the day, the Stevensons owned their own property, first in Fenner and then in the village of Cazenovia. A 1902 note in the *Cazenovia Republican* provides details of a property they purchased from Perry Crandall in the area of the Lake House hotel, now the site of Community Bank on Albany Street. John and Martha worked diligently at a variety of jobs: coachman, laundress, farmer, and day laborer to support their growing family. Martha would have eight children in all: Mary, William, Charles Edward, George, Emma, Martha, Anna, and Harley.

It seems that in the nineteenth century, as now, Cazenovians were a civic-minded lot who volunteered much free time to their community.

Despite the effort it must have taken to feed and care for such a large family, John found time to participate in community organizations like the Hayes and Wheeler political club of the 1870s. In 1884, he earned the enviable post of janitor and man of all work for the Cazenovia Seminary. "His department is properly attended to in all respects, nothing being neglected from the principal's fine horse down to the sleek and well-fed porkers," the college boasted in the *Cazenovia Republican*. John ran for the position of village trustee in 1900, which underscores both his dedication to the community as well as his confidence in his place in it. And he became an active member of GAR Knowlton Post 160 when it was formed in 1902. He was such a popular member of the community that even something as small as an increase in his Army pension was noted in the newspaper: "John Stevenson is rejoicing in the increase of his pension from $6 to $8 per month," the *Cazenovia Republican* enthused.

In a community as small as Cazenovia, it may be inevitable that bonds are formed between like-minded families, but the connection between Alberta Robbins and John Stevenson went a bit further. Perhaps they connected over their war experiences or perhaps it was through strong ties in the African American community of the village, but sometime in the 1880s John's daughter Annie met and married Alberta's son Charles. The two men, venerable veterans of a bloody war, could now bond over the happy union between their families. Unfortunately, their happiness would be short lived. Annie passed away in 1892 of consumption at the age of twenty-four.

The late 1800s, in fact, would be a time of suffering for John Stevenson's family. His wife Martha passed away after a battle with consumption in 1887, capping off a decade in which four of his children died from the dreaded disease, one infant having passed away in 1875. But despite his terrible losses, John continued to throw his energy into his work. An advertisement in an 1895 *Cazenovia Republican* enthusiastically proclaimed that John Stevenson and Thomas Williams "are prepared to dig trenches and make connections to the new sewer system promptly, and in a satisfactory manner. Give us a trial!"

When John passed away in 1914 at the age of eighty-two, it was noted in his obituary that he was "one of the oldest colored men in town." The Knowlton Post GAR once again stepped in to assist in the services and burial of one of their own at Evergreen Cemetery, just down the hill from his comrade Alberta Robbins. John left two surviving sons and a legacy of perseverance and dedication to his community.

Lynda Copper and the *History Detectives* program helped bring to light a lost heirloom from a remarkable time and place. The integration of the Knowlton Post GAR was unique among social organizations of the time, but perhaps it was not as surprising considering the inclusive nature of Cazenovia in the 1800s. John Stevenson and Alberta Robbins were much-valued members of the community, race notwithstanding. Their presence in the GAR photo is less extraordinary, and more typical, of a village that valued its citizens for their contributions, which were considerable, and their service to their country.

Historic Connection to Abraham Lincoln

Francis D. Blakeslee, Cazenovia Resident and Seminary President

Cazenovia long has been a community with connections to famous and important people. Presidents have visited and passed through; cabinet secretaries have lived here; inventors, entrepreneurs, actors, and athletes have called Cazenovia home or have connections to local residents. On the presidential side of history, it is known that sitting President Grover Cleveland spent a weekend in Cazenovia in 1887, that Theodore Roosevelt gave a speech in Cazenovia while he was a candidate for vice president in 1900, and that President Bill Clinton campaigned for his wife (first for the US Senate and then for the presidency) in Cazenovia in 1999 and 2006. But what about one of the biggest presidents of them all, Abraham Lincoln?

Lincoln never came to Cazenovia (although he did pass through Syracuse on his inaugural journey) but a man who lived here at the turn of the twentieth century had numerous historic connections to the Great Emancipator, and that man's stories and reminiscences to this day remain important firsthand information about the sixteenth president. Dr. Francis D. Blakeslee, for eight years president of Cazenovia Seminary, was known for much of his life as a national authority on Abraham Lincoln. He spoke across the country and around the world on Lincoln, wrote articles and at least two booklets, and was labeled during his life as one of the last people to see Abraham Lincoln alive on the day of his assassination. "I probably have had more contacts with Mr. Lincoln than any man living," Blakeslee said in 1939, towards the end of his life.

20. Rev. Francis D. Blakeslee in an International News Photo in 1933, shortly after celebrating his eighty-sixth birthday at his home in Los Angeles. Courtesy of Jason Emerson.

Francis Durbin Blakeslee—an educator, clergyman, college president, scholar, and ardent prohibitionist—was born February 1, 1846, in Vestal, New York. During the Civil War, being too young to enlist without his parents' permission, he served as a quartermaster's clerk in the 50th New York engineers in 1863–64, and as a clerk in the quartermaster general's office in Washington, DC, in 1864–65. After the war, he married and had three children. He attended Wyoming Seminary in Pennsylvania and became an ordained Methodist Episcopal minister in 1870. He then attended Genesee College in Lima, which became Syracuse University by an act of the state legislature. He graduated from SU in 1872—a member of the university's first-ever graduating class, which totaled nineteen students.

Blakeslee served in numerous positions as educator, administrator, and pastor throughout his life, including as principal at East Greenwich Academy, Rhode Island, president of Iowa Wesleyan University, pastor of multiple Methodist churches, superintendent of the Anti-saloon League in New York State, and president of Cazenovia Seminary. Blakeslee traveled the world and lectured as he went. During his early years, his main topic was prohibition and the evils of alcohol. Starting in the 1920s, Blakeslee's lectures began to mix his views on temperance with his belief in Abraham Lincoln's disdain of liquor. Finally, his lectures came to focus solely on his personal recollections of Abraham Lincoln and his belief in the Great Emancipator's historical worth.

At Cazenovia College

Blakeslee became president of Cazenovia Seminary in 1900 and was the second head of the school to use the title "president" rather than the previous "principal." According to the official Cazenovia College history *Generations of Excellence*, by John Robert Greene, Blakeslee oversaw some major milestones in the seminary's existence, including the installation of electric lights on campus in 1903 and the second charter change in the seminary's history, which broadened the representation of the board of trustees to include alumni and the general public. This was the first time non-Methodists were allowed on the board.

Blakeslee's tenure also included the opening of the seminary to local high school students, since the Cazenovia Union Free School District no. 10 had no such facilities. This was done as part of a plan to attract more students to the seminary itself. Blakeslee "achieved a measure of success as president, despite his decidedly hands-off approach to management," according to Greene. Blakeslee was, however, "an absentee president" who "spent most of his time on the road, giving lectures—more often than not about Lincoln or the evils of alcohol." Blakeslee resigned on March 14, 1908, moved to Binghamton, and became the local superintendent of the Anti-saloon League.

Blakeslee may have left Cazenovia in 1908, but he maintained his connection to the community for the rest of his life. He returned to Cazenovia more than once to visit friends, speak at the seminary, or preach. In June 1927, for example, he gave his lecture on "Personal Recollections of Abraham Lincoln" instead of the usual formal sermon on the Sunday night of Commencement Week, according to the *Cazenovia Republican*. Blakeslee also submitted multiple articles to the *Cazenovia Republican* through the years in which he detailed his national and world travels as well as his connections to Abraham Lincoln. In the 1920s, after he moved to California, he wrote articles about his visit to Lincoln's Home in Illinois and his travels in Australia and Japan, and multiple letters about California life and history, as well as multiple articles about his recollections of Abraham Lincoln.

In one of his private memorandum books, Blakeslee recalled meeting Methodist Bishop Frederick T. Keeney in Soochow, China, where Blakeslee preached for the bishop, Keeney being too ill to do it. "We were closely associated during eight years, 1900–1908, of my presidency of Cazenovia seminary, he being a member of the board of trustees. I preached for him several times and was a guest in his home," Blakeslee wrote. "It was at his suggestion that I tarried on Monday following my preaching on Christian Education in the Hedding Church [in Elmira], of which he was pastor, to see a young man to persuade him to enter Cazenovia Seminary. The young man was Harry E. Woolever, who since has become so prominent in Methodism [for years as editor of *The Christian Advocate* weekly newspaper]. He found his wife among the students of the seminary."

The *Cazenovia Republican* also reported in January 1934—after the paper's publisher wrote to Mrs. Blakeslee for information—that Reverend Blakeslee had been struck and nearly killed by an automobile while crossing the street, but was recovering. By the end of that year, Blakeslee had recovered and made what appears to have been his final visit to Cazenovia. In September, he attended the graduation exercises for Syracuse

University and gave the prayer, and the next day he traveled to Cazenovia, where he preached in the Methodist church.

In 1945, three years after Blakeslee's death at age ninety-six, the former Morse House on Sullivan Street was renamed Blakeslee House in honor of the former seminary president.

Blakeslee and Lincoln

But what Blakeslee was best known for during his life, and what he was most passionate about, was the life and legacy of Abraham Lincoln—including his own experiences and connections to that life and legacy. While a clerk in the War Department in 1864–65, Blakeslee saw Lincoln often, as the president was a regular visitor. But mostly the seventeen-year-old clerk watched Lincoln at public functions and in public places. He saw the president sometimes at the theater, sometimes outside the White House, sometimes at church, and sometimes at public events while Lincoln gave speeches. "While engaged in my position as a clerk in the Quartermaster General's Office, I had many excellent opportunities of seeing Lincoln, and in fact I had often met him," Blakeslee told a Binghamton newspaper in 1909.

But certain moments stood out to Blakeslee, and these he spoke of often in his Lincoln talks. One such moment was how his father, Reverend George H. Blakeslee, a Methodist minister from Binghamton, met the president and obtained his autograph. The senior Blakeslee was on leave from his pastoral duties in response to a call from the Christian Commission asking all men of the cloth to go to the front and minister to soldiers on the battlefields and in the hospitals, and to hold religious services among the troops. George did this from October 4 to November 4 and, stopping in Washington on his way home from the battlefields to visit his son Francis, decided to call upon the president at the White House.

Times were different then, and anyone for any reason could call on the president to speak with him, make a request, or simply ask to shake his hand. George Blakeslee and one of his pastoral colleagues did just that on November 2, 1864—six days before the presidential election. According to the elder Blakeslee's diary, he and his companion watched the president interact with a number of people before he got to the two ministers—and his reactions are not what modern-day people would expect of the historic figure, who is typically characterized as almost Christ-like in his kindness and forgiveness:

> Four young men approached the president who were anxious to get his aid relative to a matter which I did not understand. But Mr. Lincoln, who was seated in his chair, replied to them kindly but firmly, "I can do nothing for you." When they urged that their papers should be read, he replied, "I should not remember if I did. The papers can be put into their proper places and go through their proper channels."
>
> A lady next appeared and presented a paper. He took it out and read it and replied, "This will not do. I can do nothing for your husband." "Why not?" said the lady. "Because," said Mr. Lincoln, "he is not loyal." "But he intends to be; he wants to take the oath of allegiance." "That is the way with all who get into prison," replied the President. "I can do nothing for you." "But you would," said the lady, "if you knew my circumstances." "No, I would not. I am under no obligation to provide for the wives of disloyal husbands."

Noted Lincoln authority William E. Barton, after hearing the above story in 1936, said, "That confirms what I have long insisted upon, that Lincoln could be sufficiently stern when the facts demanded it."

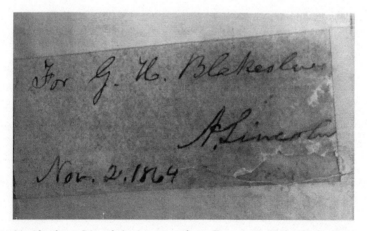

21. Abraham Lincoln's signature from Francis D. Blakeslee's autograph book. Photo by Jason Emerson. Courtesy of Kim Nunnari.

22. An 1860 presidential campaign ribbon supporting Abraham Lincoln, contained in Francis D. Blakeslee's autograph book. Photo by Jason Emerson. Courtesy of Kim Nunnari.

Lincoln scholar Michael Burlingame, author of the Lincoln Prize–winning biography *Abraham Lincoln: A Life*, agreed that the elder Blakeslee's story is a prime example of Lincoln's ability to be stern as president. "Lincoln was famously susceptible to women's appeals for mercy, but this diary entry shows that he was not always swayed by feminine supplicants," Burlingame said.

After watching Lincoln's interactions, George Blakeslee and his companion, Reverend E. W. Breckinridge (no relation to John C. Breckinridge, one of the four candidates for President in 1860, which the reverend told Lincoln when they met), watched Lincoln dispatch another widow in the same way, then shook hands with the president and Blakeslee asked for the president's signature. Lincoln "cheerfully" gave his autograph "For G.H. Blakeslee" in a memorandum book of the Christian Commission, given to George as one of the delegates of that service. "I treasure as prized possessions the leather-bound book which contains the autograph inscription in Lincoln's own hand, and my father's diary relating how he secured this precious memento that memorable day," Francis wrote in a 1927 pamphlet, *How My Father Secured Lincoln's Autograph*. In a 1936 article he wrote for the *Cazenovia Republican* newspaper, Blakeslee stated, "The ink is as black as the day it was written."

Francis then went to visit the president as an official visitor himself on January 2, 1865, with two women from his boardinghouse. "Shook his paw with gusto," Francis wrote in his diary. Little did he know that he would witness some of the seminal moments in the nation's history shortly thereafter.

Blakeslee's Recollections

Francis Blakeslee's Lincoln recollections have been quoted by multiple scholars over the years, most notably in the 1945 book *Intimate Memories of Lincoln* by Rufus Rockwell Wilson. But Blakeslee wrote his own twenty-seven-page monograph called *Personal Recollections and Impressions of Abraham Lincoln*, which contains basically the same information—and these stories are the ones he told over and over again to audiences across the world for at least fifty years.

Three months after meeting the president, Blakeslee was present for what would become Lincoln's last speech before his death, which he delivered from a second-story window of the White House. "It was about twenty minutes long and related to the problems confronting the nation at that crisis of its history, and may be found today among his published writings," Blakeslee wrote. Another member of the audience that night was the actor John Wilkes Booth, who, when he heard the president say he would be in favor of allowing Blacks who had served in the Union army to vote, exclaimed, "By God, I will put him through. That is the last speech he will ever make."

Blakeslee also saw Lincoln on the afternoon of April 14, 1865—the day Lincoln was assassinated. Blakeslee and a few of his friends had gone to the Navy Yard to admire the ironclad ships damaged in the battle at Fort Fisher, and which were docked for repairs. As the friends stood on a platform in the Yard, the president and Mrs. Lincoln drove up in their carriage and stopped at the opposite end of the platform. "We saluted, and the salute was returned," Blakeslee wrote. He also told a correspondent in 1910 that it was between five and six o'clock that day that he saw the Lincolns at the Navy Yard. "He and Mrs. Lincoln came there in their carriage on their afternoon drive. They came within a rod or two of where I was and I saluted him," Blakeslee wrote. He also wrote that in later years he was told by Lincoln scholars that the "disputed question" of where the Lincolns actually took their final carriage ride on that fateful day seems to hinge on his own testimony, with nobody apparently knowing that they even went to the Navy Yard until Blakeslee made it known.

That night, April 14, Blakeslee went to bed early in his lodging just down the street from Ford's Theater. And, despite the noise and crowds out on the street that night as the president was shot and lay dying in a boardinghouse on 14th Street, Blakeslee slept through the entire event. The next morning, he went to his usual restaurant for breakfast and noticed it was unusually quiet. "While the waitress was filling my order, the only other man at my table turned his daily papers—and then I read the black headlines telling me of the awful event of the night before," he wrote. "My father, living hundreds of miles away . . . knew of the tragedy before I did." While Lincoln's body lay in state in the White House, Blakeslee stood in line for hours and eventually got in. He stood by the casket and "looked into the cold face of him whom I had saluted in life a few hours previously." As a civil servant, Blakeslee also watched and participated in the grand funeral procession of the president.

Blakeslee also spent two days attending the military trial of the assassination conspirators in the Old Capitol Prison and, six days after John Wilkes Booth was killed by Union troops, Blakeslee met the soldier who killed the assassin, Boston Corbett. "He told me that the pistol with which he had shot Booth, and for which he had been offered over $1,000, had been stolen," Blakeslee wrote. Coincidentally, more than thirty years later, Blakeslee serendipitously met more people with direct connections to the Abraham Lincoln, including Lincoln's only surviving son, Robert. When Blakeslee became president of Iowa Wesleyan University in 1898, the president of the board that elected him (and the university's first president), former US Senator James Harlan, had been a personal friend of President Lincoln and had been named a cabinet member shortly before the assassination. Harlan was also the father-in-law of Robert T. Lincoln, the oldest and only surviving son of Abraham and Mary Lincoln. When Harlan died in 1899, Blakeslee spoke at the funeral in the college chapel. During the funeral, he met Robert Lincoln and his wife, Mary Harlan Lincoln, and, a few years later, interviewed Robert in Chicago when Lincoln was president of the Pullman Car Company.

Blakeslee's Final Years

Francis Blakeslee was a prolific writer, speaker, and traveler. After moving with his wife to California in the 1920s, Blakeslee crisscrossed the country preaching, and speaking about prohibitionism and Abraham Lincoln. It was in the 1920s that Blakeslee printed his two Lincoln-related pamphlets, and during that decade and the next he continually submitted articles to the *Cazenovia Republican* and numerous other newspapers. For its part, the *Cazenovia Republican* kept tabs on Blakeslee as well. Practically every October, the newspaper printed a story mentioning Blakeslee's birthday and, often, how he was celebrating it in California. Articles in the paper about Blakeslee had titles such as "Birthday Guest List Notables" (1929), "Former President Blakeslee of the Cazenovia Seminary . . . Tells of His Trip East" (1934) and "Ex-Cazenovia Seminary Head Still Excels as Wood Cutter" (1939). The latter article discussed how ninety-three-year-old Blakeslee was "the champion wood cutter in his neighborhood." By the 1930s and early 1940s, Blakeslee was known around the country not only as a Lincoln scholar and lecturer, but as the oldest living person to have met Abraham Lincoln, shaken his hand, heard him speak, seen the funeral, and more. He was also known as the oldest living member of the first-ever graduating class of Syracuse University.

When Blakeslee died in 1942 at age ninety-six, the news was carried in numerous newspapers across the United States, particularly in towns where Blakeslee lived and worked, such as Potsdam, Cazenovia, Syracuse, Binghamton, and Los Angeles. "Another chapter in American history closed yesterday with the death of Dr. Francis Durbin Blakeslee, 96, believed to be the last remaining person to have seen Abraham Lincoln the day he was assassinated," stated the *Los Angeles Times* in its news coverage. The *Cazenovia Republican* and *Syracuse Herald Journal* both reported that Blakeslee's talks on Lincoln, and the two pamphlets of reminiscences he published, had been heard and read by thousands of people.

In his funeral eulogy, Reverend Elmer Ellsworth Helms said Francis Blakeslee was the richest man he had ever known—he was rich in friends and family, in service and culture, in ancestry and years. "The measure of his years was almost the measure of a century," Helms stated. "When he was born, John Quincy Adams, sixth president, was still living and a member of Congress. . . . There have been forty presidential elections. He could have voted in nineteen of them—only one less than half. He saw twenty-two of the forty-eight states come into the Union. . . . When he was born the steamboat was still in its experimental stage . . . he was ten years old when the first railroad reached Chicago. . . . Of the 31,692 persons who names occur in *Who's Who in America*, only one was born before Dr. Blakeslee." In his later years, Francis Blakeslee often bragged about his entry in *Who's Who in America*—not so much because he was in there, but because his two sons were also in there with him. "I am very doubtful if there is another father and all his sons in that book," he wrote to a correspondent in 1910.

Blakeslee died surrounded by family, and an impressive family it was. He had three children: George, Albert, and Theodora. George Hubbard Blakeslee, PhD, was a world-renowned scholar on international relations, professor at Clark University, prolific author, advisor to presidents, and world traveler. Albert Francis Blakeslee was a world-renowned botanist and geneticist, and professor at Smith College.

To sum up Francis Blakeslee's life would take up vast amounts of space, and the articles about him in his final years and at his death have long lists of his accomplishments and organizational memberships. Perhaps the best look at Blakeslee was printed in February 1942, seven months before he passed away, in the *Los Angeles Times* (and reprinted in the Potsdam *Herald-Recorder* newspaper). The article shows Blakeslee, despite his advanced age, living his life as he always did. According to a family friend, who visited the Blakeslees, she found him "seated in his easy chair writing an essay on 'My Memories of Lincoln.' Dr. Blakeslee, who has given hundreds of lectures on Lincoln, no longer is able to give public addresses, but he continues to write his memoirs of the statesman." That night, Blakeslee was honored at a Syracuse University Alumni of Southern California dinner, after which he attended—you guessed it—a lecture on Abraham Lincoln.

Lucia Zora Card,
"The Bravest Woman in the World"

Cazenovia can boast of more than its fair share of notable residents. Senators, writers, and artists have all called the village home, but rarely has there been as vibrant and unique a personality as that of Lucia Zora Card. Known as "The Bravest Woman in the World," she stunned the nation with feats of daring and expertise under the big top of the circus. Women of her time lived by strict rules, but Zora ignored them all, choosing instead a life orchestrating elephant, lion, and tiger performances unlike anything that had ever been attempted.

Born in 1877, to "comfortably fixed" parents Milton E. and Myra Card of 42 Nelson Street, she began her life in the way of many well-to-do Cazenovians: an excellent education with plans to marry and settle into upper class society. In her autobiography *Sawdust and Solitude*, Zora claims her father named her for a package boat he encountered on his way back from an Arctic excursion. While this may be true, local records identify at least three other Zoras in the area, making it a fairly popular name, and she was more likely named Lucia for her grandmother.

Milton E. Card was a principal member of the Stone, Marshall & Card clock manufacturers and later of the Cruttenden & Card firm, which manufactured flying glass targets for marksmen. Milton's glass ball trap was patented in 1879 and became popular among sportsmen, bolstering Milton's reputation and bottom line. He and Myra were active and influential members of Cazenovia society; Milton served as chief engineer for the Fire Department and as a justice of the peace. The Cards began making trips to the Indian River area of Florida shortly after Zora was born, and in 1882 purchased land there to establish a pineapple plantation. During

23. Lucia Zora Card, animal tamer and circus performer, poses with Trilby the elephant for a Sells-Floto Circus promotional photo in 1916. Courtesy of the Library of Congress.

these early years, Zora remained in Cazenovia, attending the Cazenovia Seminary from age ten until she turned eighteen in 1895.

Zora recounts her formative years in Cazenovia as a time of struggle against conventional expectations. Her parents educated her to become a society matron, but Zora had other ideas. "Against this cut-and-dried existence I instinctively rebelled even before I had reached my teens," she later wrote. When a shabby circus made its way through town, young Zora followed the little elephant in the troupe with fascination, making a tracing of its footprint in the dirt. She marks this as the watershed moment when she found her life's ambition: to perform with circus animals. But for an upper-class young Cazenovian, a circus career was out of the question. So, she made her way through the Cazenovia Seminary and "endured the 'amo, amas, amat' of Latin, the intricacies of French and the guttural sounds of German; I struggled through the theological course, which Cazenovia's Seminary dictated, and pounded energetically at a piano under the tutelage of a pathetically conscientious music master," she recalled. Although she had to set aside her circus dreams for a while, Zora was still able to indulge her love of performance. It is noted in the *Cazenovia Republican* of June 1890, when Zora was thirteen, that she rode atop the Ledyard Hose Company's hose cart during the Fireman's Convention parade in a beautiful costume, entertaining the crowds. By the time Zora reached eighteen, however, her eyes were turned away from Cazenovia toward greater ambitions.

She traveled south after leaving the seminary to visit her parents on their plantation in Fort Pierce, Florida. An Indian River newspaper from 1898 describes a performance for a local fundraiser, in which Zora danced and sang, draped in a Cuban flag promoting funds for local road development. It was during her time in Florida that she auditioned and won a place with the Wilbur Kirwin Opera Company, a comic opera group that traveled throughout the south and east. Milton and Myra Card approved of her attachment to the group, "looking upon a position in opera as a distinct achievement," but they "viewed my real ambition [for the circus] as equally as great a disgrace." She was well on her way to national acclaim, and her performances were praised in articles throughout the country. An 1899 *New Orleans Telegram* article describes the dancing of "Madame Zora" as she was known, as "poetry in motion" and "one of the cleverest and most artistic dancers in the country." It was noted in this article, as in many, how physically attractive Zora had become, standing nearly six feet tall according to some reports, with blonde hair and a "well formed, supple person." It seems Zora had the makings of a first-class celebrity.

With her star rising, Zora made her way to Chicago with the theatrical troupe in 1900. In January she married William Hilliard, a leading performer with the Wilbur Opera Company. Zora makes no mention of William in her autobiography, nor is he named in any of the frequent articles concerning her after that date, so it is assumed their marriage was short lived. An unsuccessful marriage would soon be the least of Zora's concerns, however.

In October 1900, Zora became a national media sensation when she shot, perhaps fatally (although newspaper reports never said if he lived or died), an unscrupulous theater agent in Chicago. According to

contemporary reports, William Phelon, press agent at the Trocadero Theatre where Zora was engaged, made inappropriate advances towards her,
ultimately putting his feelings into writing in the form of a lascivious
letter. With characteristic sensibility and levelheadedness, Zora "did not
propose to place myself in his clutches that he might by false statements
disgrace me before my parents and friends." She turned the letter over
to police, who prosecuted Phelon for sending obscene material through
the mail.

A friend of Phelon, Joseph Pazen, also an agent, began pressuring
Zora to leave the area to keep her from testifying before a grand jury.
When she repeatedly refused, Pazen attacked Zora, attempting to strangle
and throw her down a flight of stairs. Zora, who said she would "always
go armed, carrying my pistol in the bosom of my dress," managed to
shoot Pazen in the stomach and call police. She was detained during the
investigation but ultimately no charges were filed. While it was never
reported whether Pazen succumbed to his wound, the press created a
media frenzy, printing the story throughout the country and portraying
Zora as either a femme fatale or honorable woman wronged, depending
on the publication. Zora herself seemed unfazed by the histrionics and
wrote confidently to her parents that "I shall be exempt from the charge
on self-defense so there is no cause for you to worry or fear any consequences for I am perfectly justified."

Understandably, Zora makes no mention of this period in *Sawdust and
Solitude*. Instead, she writes that she ran away "coldly, deliberately burning my bridges behind me" to join the circus at age nineteen, leaving the
opera group in New Orleans. Zora would have been nineteen in 1896, and
there is no record of her joining the Wilbur Kirwin Opera Company until
1899. So perhaps this was her way of rearranging events to support her
narrative. Either way, by 1902, she had left the theater world and taken
the first step toward her childhood dream by joining a small circus as
a "generally useful girl" who would dance in the ballet pieces and ride
horses during the grand entrée. Unfortunately, the small group went
broke, leaving Zora stranded and forced to work as a short-order cook
for a time. She was so determined to follow her dreams that she never
considered returning home, even during a time when she was penniless.
But while she was broke, she was not without friends. An old Cazenovia acquaintance, Jim Fitch, another circus performer, said he found her

a position with the Sells-Floto Circus. This time her position would be the culmination of her ambitions: to train and perform with animals. Her parents' reaction to this turn of events can only be guessed at, though with a daughter like Zora, perhaps it was better not to stand in her way. In *Sawdust*, Zora notes that by the time she retired from circus life, Milton and Myra "had learned that the circus is not the terrible thing it is supposed to be, but a human sort of affair after all," which points at least to their resignation if not encouragement.

Zora's career with Sells-Floto began similarly to her last circus experience: she would be a generally useful girl and ride horses, dance, and perform in other acts. Animal training at this time was almost exclusively a male affair; women were considered too delicate to handle the work. But Zora, with determination and bravado, convinced the circus owner to give her a try. She was, after all, no lightweight and described herself as: "160 pounds of strong muscle, bone and sinew." She was assisted in this new endeavor by the circus superintendent, Fred Alispaw, a handsome animal trainer five years her junior. Fred saw in Zora a talented performer who shared his respect for the animals of the menagerie. Together they would choreograph and arrange some of Zora's most daring performances.

Professional respect between Fred and Zora would shortly blossom into love and they quietly eloped, hoping to avoid fanfare. But what is a circus without hullaballoo? The pair began a performance shortly after their elopement, thinking they had pulled off the trick, when they noticed that the lead elephant in the parade wore a banner reading: "Just Married" and was trailing old shoes from its tail. The circus band struck up "The Wedding March" and the crowds tossed rice at the couple while the clowns pantomimed a wedding ceremony. So much for subterfuge.

Circus life fulfilled Zora's every childhood dream. Fred taught her to tend to sick and injured animals, even wrestling sick tigers through treatment and cajoling recalcitrant elephants. Together they pioneered a new way of dealing with the animals. Zora explained that rather than dominating the beasts, she learned to communicate with them and put them at ease. She was convinced that an animal's fear of the trainer was far greater than the reverse. It was her ability to sympathize with and respect the animals in her care that allowed her to perform her most daring acts in the ring. She notes that an elephant "only obeys that which creates respect" and that "if an elephant loves you, he loves you with his heart, soul, and hide." She had a particularly close relationship with an elephant named Snyder. She describes how the hulking bull saved her life many times by protecting her from trampling feet or by holding her gingerly in his trunk. She believed he loved her as a child loves its mother, despite their difference in size. When Zora and Fred left the circus years later, Snyder suffered heartbreak, and eventually went berserk under mistreatment and was shot. Zora would have his hide displayed in her home for years to come as a reminder of the bond they shared.

After working with the menagerie for some time and even handraising a pair of baby elephants, Zora announced to Fred that she wanted to create "the most spectacular elephant act in show business," to impress their boss. "Don't want much," he is said to have ironically replied. Nevertheless, Fred assisted her and together they created a circus sensation. She gained fame as "a most daring and successful wild animal educator and the only woman handling an entire herd of elephants," according to a *Cazenovia Republican* article. Zora's astonishing show included an elephant waltz, wherein the pachyderms "whirl about rapidly in the ring in time to music." During the performance, the animals "looked neither to the right nor to the left" while Zora leaped about beneath them, narrowly avoiding their enormous feet, "sliding into a safety zone just in time to miss being sandwiched between two of the hulking beasts when they would crash together with the noise of a pair of freight cars in a railroad collision." As astonishing and dangerous as this was, it was only the beginning for Zora. She would choreograph elephant shows in which the animals lifted themselves into a pyramid over her, or she would have an animal lift her in its trunk and send her flying. Though Zora makes note of the injuries she sustained in practice, she remained undaunted in her task. She describes herself at this time as possessing "a strength which some men might have envied." For her bravado she was dubbed by a rival show owner with the epithet that would follow her for the rest of her life: The Bravest Woman in the World. And strength and bravery she would need as she moved into a more dangerous animal arena.

Zora took her animal training skills a step further when she decided to work with a mixed group of lions and tigers, a feat no other woman had attempted. In a 1920 *Saturday Evening Post* article, she was asked whether she would be willing to step into a ring with a mixed group. Quietly confident, as ever, she responded, "Well, don't know that I would regard it as a picnic exactly, but it's all in the game. I'd do it if I had to." And do it she did. She successfully trained the animals—all still in possession of their claws and teeth—to walk a tightrope and to ride horseback around the ring. This was not without her share of hiccups, however. In one hair-raising instance, she was working with an irritable tigress when it leapt upon her and "an instant later I was borne to the ground, struggling against the weight of a four-hundred-pound assailant, while the burning of flesh told of the incision of swift-working claws at fully a dozen places on my body!" Fred managed to rescue her and with characteristic calmness, she excused the tigress' behavior as the result of a headache. Undaunted, she continued to work with the big cats, though not without further scrapes. In another incident, a tiger fastened its teeth into the back of her neck, and she was only saved by her uniform cape, which acted as a buffer and saved her life, though she walked away with lifelong scars.

During her years with the circus, Zora spent her time away from the ring recording her adventures. Around 1916 or 1917, she began publishing articles in leading magazines such as the *Saturday Evening Post*, *Red Book*, *Collier's*, and others. These articles contributed to Zora's reputation as "The Bravest Woman in the World" and introduced her to an audience beyond the circus ring. It was at this time that she and Fred determined to retire from circus life and pursue a life of homesteading far from the "land of the white tops," as she called it. World War I was raging and Zora describes a desire to help support the war effort by raising cattle. The Alispaws set out for Fortification, Colorado, in December of 1917 to begin life as ranchers, leaving their friends, and the animals they had grown to love, behind. Zora and Fred put their strength and efforts into raising cattle and growing their feed in a rugged wilderness far from the company of family or friends. According to *Sawdust*, it was the biggest challenge of the pair's lives. While she may not have rejoined the circus life "for all the gold that is beneath the moon," homestead life would take its toll on the Alispaws. Fred is rumored to have hidden their guns in a snowbank to protect Zora from harming herself during the first grueling winter. The solitude of homestead life had become its own burden and Zora's mental health was pushed to its limits.

Perhaps to enliven her days or possibly to rekindle some of the fame she had left behind, Zora began publishing her memoirs in the *Ladies Home Journal* in serialized form in 1924. The series, under the title "The Bravest Woman in the World," was extremely popular and led Zora to consolidate the tales into what would become her autobiography, *Sawdust and Solitude*, later in the year. Cazenovia's public library received an edition in 1928 that is still available today.

Despite relative success with the cattle venture, Fred and Zora decided to relocate from Colorado to Fort Pierce, Florida, around 1927. Zora's parents had built a magnificent home, known as "Fair View," in the area in 1914 which served as a base for their pineapple and citrus operations. The Alispaws' reasons for leaving Colorado remain unclear, but considering the difficulties Zora experienced living in isolation, a desire to be close to family may have contributed to their decision. Zora's father, Milton, was in poor health and passed away, with Zora by his side, later in 1927. Myra, Zora's mother, was also ill and would pass away in 1932.

The move to Florida brought yet more changes to Zora's life. In an ironic turn, she took on the role of society matron she had avoided all her life. She joined the Fort Pierce Woman's Club and the Democratic Club, and chaired the Indian welfare division of the Florida Federation of Women's Clubs, among others. She was beloved in her community and apparently never tired of recounting her circus days and showing off the scars she had acquired. Fort Pierce resident Edith Hoeflich Luke recalls that Zora "was invited to everything. She showed the ladies her scratches and scars from training animals and so on. She was a very popular person." The Alispaws decorated the house on Indian River Drive with mementos of their days under the big top, hanging elephant hides, artifacts, and mementos around the sprawling estate. Unfortunately, Zora would not spend many years in her Florida home. She passed away on November 11, 1936, at age fifty-nine, possibly from cancer, and was buried in an unmarked grave at Fort Pierce's Riverview Memorial Park.

Zora's death was met with sadness in her childhood community of Cazenovia. Many of her friends remained in the village and many more had come to know of her through her fame and her autobiography. Recollections of her time in the village were printed, including that of Edward Farley, who would himself attain fame playing professional baseball. He recalled "our attempts to get into the barn to watch Zora Card of Nelson

Street practice on the trapeze" during the circus's stay in town. Shortly after she passed away, the *Cazenovia Republican* printed a poem in her honor. It reads:

> I sing farewell to Zora Card.
> She lent a little dab of color
> And life here would be dull or duller
> Had there been no Zora Card.
>
> Her later life seems almost hard—
> For she joined at length a circus;
> With lions and elephants, 'twould irk us
> And we would think our life ill starred.
>
> Not she, she gloried in her "cats,"
> Taught them tricks and soon became
> The "Sawdust Queen," rose to fame
> The "Bravest Woman" and so that's
>
> One good reason, light or hard.
> Besides she lent a dab of color
> And life here would be dull or duller
> Had there been no Zora Card.
>   (November 15, 1936)

For more than eighty years, the Card family's graves remained unmarked. It was known that Milton, Myra, and Zora had been buried in the Card family plot in Fort Pierce's Riverview Memorial Park, but the location of their graves was not identified in any way. It was not until 2010 that the mystery was solved when Fort Pierce mayor Linda Hudson and her sister Jean Ellen Wilson tracked down the family's genealogical records and located three unmarked burial plots in the cemetery. They discovered that Zora was buried at the feet of her parents on a hill overlooking the Indian River Lagoon. Why Fred Alispaw had not erected a monument at her death, however, is left to rumor. Fred was considered parsimonious by relatives and it is possible he felt the outlay of money was unnecessary. In 2017, *Indian River Magazine* sponsored the dedication of a memorial grave marker for Zora, with a small plaque bearing the words: Lucia Zora 1877–1936 'The Bravest Woman in the World.' Movies and books continue to romanticize circus life even while the idea of running away to join the circus has faded for most children. But for Zora, the idea became a reality far outshining any work of fiction. For a young girl from Cazenovia, Lucia Zora Card had come a very long way.

When President Cleveland
Came to Cazenovia

It seems almost everyone in Cazenovia knows that at one point in the village's history President Grover Cleveland came for a brief visit in 1887. Some people even know that President and Mrs. Cleveland held a reception at Lorenzo, the local home of his secretary of the treasury Charles S. Fairchild, and spent the night there. Other than those few details, the visit of a sitting US president to the small Cazenovia community appears to be relatively unknown but, at the time, it was one of the biggest events to ever happen to this small village.

Stephen "Big Steve" Grover Cleveland lived in Fayetteville with his family from 1841 to 1850, when he was ages four to thirteen. He returned for two years from ages fifteen to seventeen to work as a store clerk. He settled as an adult in Buffalo, where he practiced law. In 1863, he was drafted to serve in the Civil War but chose to hire a substitute instead so he could continue to work and support his family.

As a politician, "Big Steve" (who weighed over 250 pounds), a Democrat, was elected a city ward supervisor in Buffalo and became assistant district attorney for Erie County. In 1870, Cleveland was elected sheriff of Erie County and in 1881, at the age of forty-four, he was elected mayor of Buffalo. Cleveland was a reformer who believed in hard work, merit, and efficiency. As mayor he exposed graft and corruption in the city's municipal services, vetoed dozens of pork-barrel appropriations, and earned a reputation as an industrious worker. Only one year after becoming mayor, Democrats named him as their candidate for governor, a position he won in 1882. He carried his political philosophy of honesty, hard work, and reform to Albany, where he was given the nickname "Governor Veto" because of all the special privilege and pork barrel legislation he rejected.

Less than two years after being elected to lead his state, he became the first Democrat since 1856 elected to the presidency.

The main political questions during Cleveland's time as president centered mainly on contemporary issues such as monetary policy (whether the United States should be on the gold standard or the silver standard), tariff policy, Chinese immigration, and race relations in the south (where he opposed racial integration of schools). During his second term, he had to deal with the economic depression of 1893. As president, Cleveland's greatest successes are considered to be his forceful championing of civil service and ethics reform in government, and the executive power he restored to what had become a weak presidential office subservient to the Congress. Of course, Cleveland is best known today as the president with the strange name (Grover) and for being the only president in American history to be elected to two nonconsecutive terms (1884–88 and 1892–96).

When President Cleveland visited Cazenovia in 1887, he was fifty years old, in the middle of his first term in the White House, and a newlywed. Cleveland married Frances Folsom, age twenty-one, in 1886—the first president ever to marry in the White House. During the summer of 1887, the couple took their honeymoon as a trip touring the western and southern states of the Union, during which they stopped in Upstate New York specifically to visit the village of Clinton, where the president spent some of his childhood, and which was celebrating its centennial. The Clevelands' trip to Clinton ultimately was updated to include a visit to his childhood home of Fayetteville, during which the president's secretary of the treasury, Charles Fairchild, invited the Clevelands to stay overnight at his wife's family home, Lorenzo, in the village of Cazenovia. The story of Cleveland's visit to Cazenovia is extensively detailed in multiple primary sources, including the Cazenovia, Fayetteville, and Syracuse newspapers and the diary of twenty-one-year-old Mary Fitzhugh Ledyard, a cousin of Mrs. Helen Lincklaen Fairchild, who was present for the president's entire visit.

Notices were published in the July 14 issue of the *Cazenovia Republican* announcing the president's visit, encouraging village residents to keep the streets clean, to hang bunting and decorations on their homes, and to participate in the planned lake fete. There was also a notice from Mrs. Ledyard Lincklaen inviting residents to attend the public reception for the Clevelands at Lorenzo from 4 to 6 p.m. on July 18. According to newspaper

President and Mrs Cleveland

24. President and Mrs. [Grover] Cleveland, c. 1893. Courtesy of the Library of Congress.

coverage, the village was patriotically decorated as never before, with many villagers starting the process as much as a week before the president's arrival. "Politics and party lines, for the nonce, were entirely obliterated and each vied with another in their endeavors to honor such distinguished guests," the newspaper stated.

The presidential party arrived in Cazenovia at 11:30 a.m., Monday, July 18, where it was greeted by Secretary and Mrs. Fairchild, President of the Village L. W. Ledyard, the village trustees, a procession of village officials, fire and police officers, the Canastota band, and scores of local residents from all walks of life. When they emerged from the train, the president wore a black suit, black necktie, and a tall white hat, while his wife wore a silk traveling dress of "quiet colors" under a black cloak. Instead of loud and raucous cheers when the presidential party arrived, the crowd was quiet, subdued, and respectful. As the grand procession of carriages and people moved from the train station up William Street to Lincklaen Avenue, to Albany Street to Lorenzo, village residents continued to welcome the president with solemn dignity. "The streets were thronged, but there was little applause, the populace demonstrating their respect by removing their hats. The president bowed right and left, and occasionally removed his hat to a group of ladies," reported the *Cazenovia Republican*.

The Clevelands and the Fairchilds drove straight to Lorenzo, where they were greeted by Mrs. Ledyard Lincklaen, were treated to lunch, and then relaxed briefly in the mansion garden before the public reception. During this time, Lizzie Ledyard presented Mrs. Cleveland with a George Washington cup and saucer in a case made from the wood of the tree under which Cazenovia founder John Lincklaen pitched his tent. "Mrs. Cleveland expressed delight at the gift and declared she would always treasure it," according to the *Cazenovia Republican*. The president was given the bedroom in the front of the house as his chamber, which overlooked the vast front lawn and grand view of Cazenovia Lake.

The *New York Times* correspondent, in describing Lorenzo (which he mistakenly called "Lincklaen") for his readers, wrote, "Its broad acres of lawn, its magnificent garden, containing rare and beautiful flowers and trees and shaded walks, make it one of the most picturesque spots in one of the prettiest villages throughout the length and breadth of the Empire State." He continued: "Of Lincklaen, the beautiful home of Secretary and

Mrs. Fairchild, the president and Mrs. Cleveland cannot say enough in praise. Its history is the history of the village of Cazenovia."

The public reception was unlike anything ever seen before in Cazenovia. The *Cazenovia Republican* reported that thousands of villagers and visitors began crowding around the Lorenzo grounds, sitting on the stone perimeter wall two hours before the reception began. So many people had descended on the village to see the president that the newspaper stated, "Cazenovia seemed a miniature metropolis." During the public reception, the president, Mrs. Cleveland, and Mrs. Fairchild stood in line in the hallway and greeted visitors as they came in through the front door and made their way through the house and out the back into the garden. A special police force was stationed at the front door of Lorenzo to hold back a rush from the mob and prevent the president and first lady from being crushed to death. The visitors entered the mansion at about twenty-five per minute, and the president greeted everybody with a handshake and a "How do you do!"

According to Mary Ledyard in her diary, four thousand people greeted the president and went through Lorenzo in two hours. "I never thought to see such a mob as infested Aunt Lincklaen's well-ordered grounds and fought for admittance at her door step. The jam about the piazza was terrible and several women fainted. . . . and by six o'clock the president and Mrs. Cleveland seemed quite exhausted," Ledyard wrote. The presidential party ate dinner at Lorenzo that evening, and then witnessed the grand lake fete from the grounds of the Owaghena Club. According to the Fayetteville *Weekly Recorder*, the evening included "a magnificent display of fireworks on the lake which resembled a scene from a fairy land. A fleet of 100 boats illuminated by Japanese lanterns, rafts with Greek fire, bonfires along the lakeshore, sky rockets, etc., etc., made the lake a scene of beauty and grandeur seldom witnessed."

The next morning, the president and his wife traveled nearly two hours by carriage down East Lake Road, onto the Seneca Turnpike (now Route 173) and down Salt Springs Road to Fayetteville, where the president visited his childhood home, lunched with his sister Mary Hoyt at her home on the corner of Elm and Manlius streets, and was honored by that village with decorations, cheers, and adulating crowds. The speeches and public reception that afternoon occurred in Clinton Park, where the president was addressed by boyhood friends and shook hands for almost two hours, going at a rate of forty-four people per minute, according to Fayetteville Village Historian Barbara S. Rivette, author of the booklet, *Grover Cleveland: Fayetteville's Hometown Boy*. Although the president did not give a speech, he gave a few brief remarks during which he recalled childhood scenes and friends and marveled at the changes to the village. "All of these memories have gone with me through my life," he said.

The president left Fayetteville at around 3 p.m. to drive back to Cazenovia to catch the train to Washington. This time, the party's route took them through the village of Manlius, where the president stopped and gave a short speech. "I have been more affected by the receptions of the past few days than by all other receptions that have been tendered me put together," he said. "This has been one of the pleasantest days of my life. Now that I must leave, on finding that I must again go to my official duties, I do it with the greatest regret, for I would linger long among these scenes from my boyhood. I hope in days to come to see you often, and I promise that I shall hereafter be a more dutiful son to Fayetteville and to Manlius."

The presidential party then continued their drive to Cazenovia, which they reached at about 5 p.m. They relaxed and had tea in the Lorenzo garden for ninety minutes until the presidential couple had to board their train for the return to Washington. During that hour and a half, the president helped transplant a young white pine tree from the woods around Lorenzo into the garden behind the house at the request of Mrs. Ledyard Lincklaen, "a venerable lady of almost seventy years," described the *New York Times*. "Little George Ledyard, a lad of eleven years, the grandson of Mrs. Lincklaen, helped them as they tucked away its roots in the ground," stated the story. Mary Ledyard's diary contains a more honest assessment of the event, stating that "little George" helped the president plant a tree "and was not at all overcome by the honor."

At 6:30 p.m. on Tuesday, July 19, after tea, President and Mrs. Cleveland boarded the train at the Cazenovia station which took them back to Washington, DC. The *New York Times* correspondent wrote, "It was with regret that the party said goodbye to the secretary's home and turned their faces toward Washington." In her diary, Mary Ledyard declared the visit a success, and stated that the president "came and saw and conquered—that is Mrs. Cleveland did for she took all hearts by storm." The *Cazenovia Republican* stated that the president's visit was "a day long to be remembered" in the village, while Village President Ledyard issued a thank-you notice to the residents for making the presidential visit so successful. "The visit of so many famous persons is an event of unusual interest, and only such a combined effort as marked the occasion would have made it so agreeable to all," Ledyard wrote. "Too much cannot be said in praise of the extreme quiet and uniform courtesy that characterized residents and strangers, and it is a proud record that no arrests were made for any disorder or intoxication in a vast crowd of people."

Shortly after the president's visit, Mrs. Lincklaen had the "Grover Cleveland Tree," as it subsequently became known, transplanted from the back garden into the woods on the western side of the mansion, and a memorial stone marker placed next to it. The tree has grown there ever since, and stands there to this day. Interestingly, the tree was widely believed to have been blown down in a hurricane about 1955. On October 11, 1972, however, the *Cazenovia Republican* published an article stating that the tree was in fact still alive and on the Lorenzo property, and quoted Mrs. Arthur Diefendorf of Lincklaen Street, who said the late George Ledyard had shown her and her husband the tree in 1966. Next to the article was published a photo of the Grover Cleveland Tree under the headline, "We Found It!" The caption read that Lorenzo caretaker Benton Block had showed the tree to the editor of the *Cazenovia Republican*.

President and Mrs. Cleveland never again visited Cazenovia, as far as is known, although reprints and summaries of reports of the presidential visit of 1887 have been constantly printed in the *Cazenovia Republican* for more than one hundred years. In 1937—the fiftieth anniversary of the visit—the *Cazenovia Republican* printed a front-page story about it; in 1987, the centennial of the event, more stories were printed in local newspapers and the village of Fayetteville hosted a reenactment. The Clevelands' visit remains one of the seminal moments in the history of Cazenovia village, and is also one of the major talking points during guided tours of the Lorenzo State Historic Site. While Cazenovia has seen another president visit in recent years (Bill Clinton), a US Senator (Hillary Clinton), and a Speaker of the US House of Representatives (John Boehner), modern-day security is so stringent that the people of the village will never again be able to shake hands with and speak to a sitting US president the way they did on that summer day in July 1887.

The Cazenovia Mummy, Robert Hubbard, and Generations of Interest

The community of Cazenovia is known for many things, but its most famous attribute may be the two-thousand-year-old Egyptian mummy that has been on display in the Cazenovia Public Library and Museum for over 120 years. The mummy, and the Mummy Room in which he lies, has been an object and a place of wonder, curiosity, and education for generations of children and adults, residents and visitors alike. In fact, people come from across the country and around the world just to see the Cazenovia mummy, known as "Hen." Over the past two decades, Hen has gained further notoriety after being professionally photographed, x-rayed, CAT scanned, academically studied by Egyptologists, and made the subject of a documentary film. What is known about Hen now is far more detailed—and far different—than what was known about this ancient curiosity when it arrived in Cazenovia in 1894.

The story of how a two-thousand-year-old mummy ended up in a small American village is less bizarre than it may seem to people today. Cazenovia's first library opened in 1828, but the Cazenovia Public Library as it is known today at 100 Albany Street was created in 1890. In that year, village resident Robert J. Hubbard purchased an 1830 Greek revival house formerly owned by John Williams (who created the first circulating library in Cazenovia out of his general store) and donated the building to the Cazenovia Library Society. The society fitted the building with "new bookcases, shelves and other conveniences of the most approved kind," with the circulation room, stacks, and reading rooms on the ground floor. A few years later, an upstairs room was specifically reserved as a museum for natural history specimens, objects of local interest, and a collection of Egyptian artifacts.

The Egyptian artifacts—including the mummy Hen—were gifted to the library and its museum by Hubbard, who had collected them during his nine-month Grand Tour of Egypt in 1894. During his travels, Hubbard collected items such as masks, breastplates and sandals, ushabtis, scarabs, and other objects, and purchased them with the specific intention of creating a museum upstairs in the library building. While this may sound like historical thievery today, during the Victorian era it was fashionable for wealthy Americans and Europeans to visit Egypt and bring home trunks full of souvenirs, including stones and mortar from the Great Pyramids, ancient artifacts—and even mummies.

Hubbard kept a detailed account of his travels in a journal (which still exists today), including the facts of how he purchased the mummy for his hometown. One of the first places he visited upon his arrival in Cairo in February 1894 was the pyramids. "We went first to the Sphynx and the Excavated Temple with its huge granite boulders and gazed in wonder while the '40 (centaurs) looked down on us' and then battling the filthy Beduin we were pulled up to the entrance to the Pyramids and down the steep slippery incline to the interior chamber," Hubbard wrote. "I wouldn't do it again for a fawn. It was dirty and fatiguing—once done will not be repeated." Three days later, he discovered that one could purchase a mummy for "very moderate prices" of $20 to $30. One month later, after a trip up the Nile to tour Memphis, Luxor, Karnak, Thebes, and other ancient cities, Hubbard was back in Cairo seeking a mummy "that will answer for our Caz library." On March 14, Hubbard had purchased two mummies—one that was unwrapped to see if any jewels or other treasures were hidden in the wrappings (which they were not) and one to send home to Cazenovia for the library museum.

On April 5, 1894, the *Cazenovia Republican* newspaper reported on Hubbard's purchase and the fact that it was then en route to Cazenovia. "The mummy is a fine one and in a good state of preservation," the newspaper stated. "It is in the later period when Greek art asserted itself in Egypt. Its age is somewhere about 2,000 years." The mummy arrived in Cazenovia in May 1894 but was not unpacked until Hubbard himself returned home that November. On January 31, 1895, the mummy exhibit was opened to the public and celebrated with the holding of a "mummy tea"—a tea party in the library building "at the low price of ten cents," with the proceeds to go to the library fund. The event was "a great success socially and financially," raising over $35, of which $26.40 was given to the library, according to the newspaper. "The refreshments were excellent, and everything possible was done to make the occasion a pleasant one to all who came."

The *Cazenovia Republican* also gave a detailed description of the mummy, the sarcophagus, and the other artifacts that Mr. Hubbard had brought home with him—the first such description of the village's newest resident the newspaper had printed. The report referred to Hen as "the embalmed lady," since Hubbard had been told the mummy was that of an Egyptian princess. According to the newspaper article:

> The mummy rests in the bottom of a new glass case in one of the upper rooms of the house, and to the disappointment of many people it is not entirely unwrapped. It seems that after the embalming process was finished, a hollow mask of a substance resembling paper-mache, and large enough to cover the head and shoulders, of the deceased, was slipped into position, and below this, narrow strips of cloth were wound around the body and back over the mask itself. Those windings were then covered with other windings of wider cloth, until the body became quite bulky, when it was placed in its coffin and laid away. In this case, all the wrappings except the first layer had been removed, exposing the mask, but not the face. The face of the mask is gilded, and the gilding and painting is as fresh, apparently, after the lapse of 2,000 years, as when it was first put on. The strips of cloth with which it is wound are yellow with age, and are wound on in exactly the same pattern as the familiar log-cabin bed quilt—another illustration of the fact that there is nothing new under the sun.
>
> The reason for retaining some of the coverings to the mummy was explained by the appearance of a skull on another shelf,—all that remained of another mummy unrolled in Mr. Hubbard's presence last year, the other parts of the body having crumbled on exposure to the air.
>
> On the topmost shelf of the cabinets reposes the wooden coffin in which the body has been entombed, showing no decay, the marks of saw and plane plainly visible, and showing the curious way of fastening it together with small wooden pins instead of nails. On other shelves are arranged many other funereal curios of the ancient Egyptians such as

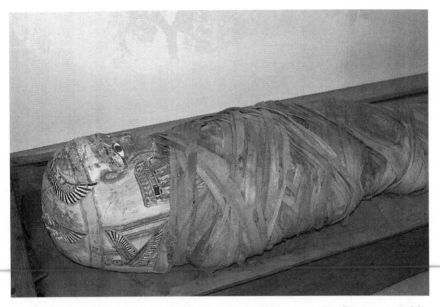

25. Cazenovia's famous mummy, Hen, in his display case in the Cazenovia Public Library in 2018. Reprinted with permission of Eagle News.

small images of Osiris, the great god and king of the underworld, covered with hieroglyphics, mummy necklaces of rude beads, tear bottle, mummied ibis and cat, images of Ra, the eagle-headed god, scarabs, etc.

And there in the Cazenovia Public Library, the mummy and the numerous other artifacts collected by Hubbard remained on public display. In May 1912, the *Cazenovia Republican* reminded its readers of the many interesting objects in the library's museum. "Chief among these curios is the Egyptian mummy, the gift of the late Mr. Hubbard. This is the one thing in Cazenovia that does not change—progress. New firms and faces are noticed by former Cazenovians coming back for a visit, but the mummy greets one with as much cordiality as upon the first meeting," the story stated.

For over a century, the mummy, explained to be a middle-aged Egyptian princess, was visited by thousands of people every year. In the 1940s, an Egyptologist at the Metropolitan Museum of Art in New York was shown photos of the Cazenovia mummy and translated the hieroglyphics on the coffin, which declared the deceased's name to be "Hen." The foot of the coffin, however, had been broken off, so "Hen" was not, in fact, the mummy's complete name, only the first syllable of the name—but Hen became the mummy's name from that day forward for Cazenovia. The mummy was x-rayed in the 1980s and again in the 1990s, with the results showing that Hen had good teeth and bones, was five feet, six inches tall, was between thirty and fifty years old, and appeared to be a female based on the roundness of the pelvic structure.

Then in 2006, Hen was taken out of the library, driven by ambulance to Crouse Hospital in Syracuse, and subjected to a CT scan. The hope was that the better medical equipment—and the three-dimensional hologram of the body inside the wrappings it would create—could tell the library staff more information about the ancient embalmed woman inside. The test results were quite revealing, showing what appeared to be a cancerous tumor in the body's left leg, and male genitalia. "How am I going to tell the third graders?" was the first thought of library executive director Betsy Kennedy. Since 2006, Hen's story has changed to say he was a young man probably in his early twenties and that he may have died from cancer. The x-rays and scans of his body are also on display in the library museum.

In December 2017, Hen made a second trip to Crouse Hospital for an MRI scan and for a biopsy of his legs and lung. The intent of the tests was to see if updated technology could reveal new and previously unknown aspects of Hen's life and death—particularly about the tumor in his leg and the prevalence of the cancer in his body. The preliminary results, announced four months later, unearthed some new facts about Hen's life and death, including his general health and some of the burial ceremonies and rituals done after his death.

While the new MRI scans are much crisper and clearer than those from 2006, the results of the lung and leg biopsies were not conclusive due to the age and resultant breakdown of the tested tissue. More tests were undertaken, however, to see if it can be ascertained if Hen had tuberculosis or a spot in his lung was some type of cancer. The biopsied tissue also was sent in 2017 to Switzerland for DNA testing to see if any new information could be gleaned from it in that way. Unfortunately, the tests were inconclusive. There were some new discoveries about Hen, however. There was what appears to be a ceramic scarab, about one-half to

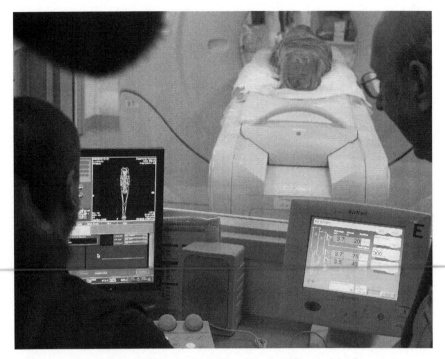

26. Hen underwent an MRI scan in 2017 at Crouse Hospital in Syracuse to see if modern technology could reveal new medical facts about the 2,000-year-old mummy. Reprinted with permission of Eagle News.

three-quarters of an inch in size, inside the mummy wrapping just above Hen's knee. Scarabs were considered good luck or bringers of healing to the ancient Egyptians, so to have placed a scarab near his knee seems to bolster the idea that Hen had knee problems, possibly cancer. While it was discovered in 2006 that Hen had what appears to be a statue inside his chest cavity, the new scans showed numerous white specks on the statue's image, which could show either paint or perhaps even writing. Also found on the new scans was the fact that Hen has severely deformed feet, with excessively high arches and hammer toes, or what could possibly be Charcot-Marie-Tooth Disorder, a neurological abnormality of the feet. What it means is that Hen might not have been able to lift his toes as he swung each foot going back to forward.

The media coverage surrounding Hen's 2017 hospital visit not only intrigued the general public but caught the interest of a Syracuse-area production company, which created a twenty-minute documentary titled "The Mummy of Cazenovia." The film explored how Hen came to be in Cazenovia, what is known about him, what occurred during the 2017 hospital visit, and what the tests showed about him medically and historically. In October 2018, the Cazenovia Public Library held a premiere party for the first showing of the film, which included tea refreshments at ten cents a cup—a recreation of the 1895 mummy tea. "It's a celebration of Hen and the culmination of many people—hospital staff, doctors, Egyptologists, library staff, and community members—coming together to have this wonderful synthesis of what we work together to explain about our 'co-worker,'" said library director Kennedy. "It's a celebration of a lot of work over many years."

To this day, visitors to the small community of Cazenovia can walk into the public library during regular hours to visit Hen, see the impressive collection of ancient Egyptian artifacts collected by Robert Hubbard over one hundred years ago and, for a while at least, immerse themselves in the wonder of the past.

Theodore Roosevelt's 1900 Campaign Whistle Stop in Cazenovia

The village of Cazenovia shone with a glowing pride for years in the aftermath of the 1887 two-day visit by sitting President Grover Cleveland. Residents also were proud that Cleveland's former treasury secretary, Charles S. Fairchild, lived in their town after he left Washington. Just thirteen years later, another nationally known figure stopped in Cazenovia, one who would also sit in the presidential chair and make an indelible mark on the country—Theodore Roosevelt.

Roosevelt visited Cazenovia on October 24, 1900, as he campaigned in support of the Republican presidential ticket for the fall election. Roosevelt, at the time governor of New York State and running mate to President William McKinley, visited Cazenovia as part of an eleven-day, two-state whistle-stop campaign tour that took him from New Jersey through Upstate New York and down to New York City. Cazenovians were notified in the October 18 issue of the *Cazenovia Republican* newspaper that Roosevelt would "pass through" Cazenovia on October 24, where he would address the people for ten minutes. According to a train schedule published in Murat Halstead's 1902 book, *The Life of Theodore Roosevelt*, Roosevelt's special campaign train started out at 11 a.m., Monday, October 22, in Weehawken, New Jersey, and did not stop until Friday, November 2, in New York City, with Roosevelt speaking an average of ten times per day. On Wednesday, October 24, Roosevelt started his day at 10 a.m. in Norwich, after which he traveled to Earlville, Cazenovia, Canastota, Oneida, Rome, Utica, and Herkimer, and ended the day back in Utica at 6:20 p.m.

When the governor's special train pulled into the Lehigh Valley Railroad Depot on William Street at approximately 11 a.m., an estimated two thousand people crowded around the station to catch a glimpse of the

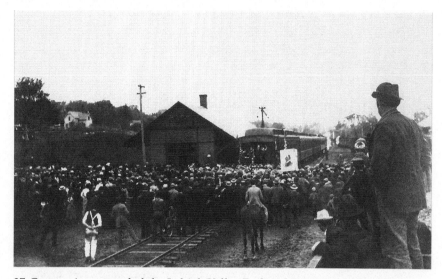

27. Cazenovians crowded the Lehigh Valley Railroad Depot on William Street to greet New York Governor and vice-presidential candidate Theodore Roosevelt in October 1900. Roosevelt visited Cazenovia as he campaigned in support of the Republican presidential ticket for the fall election. Courtesy Gene Gissin, Historic Lehigh Valley Railroad Depot, Cazenovia, New York.

Republican vice-presidential candidate. The crowd comprised people of all ages and social classes, including members of the McKinley and Roosevelt Sound Money Club, students of the Cazenovia Seminary, and pupils from the Union school, according to reporting in the *Cazenovia Republican*.

Speaking from the rear platform of his train car, Roosevelt's brief speech was a rejection of the fiscal policies of the Democrat presidential candidate William Jennings Bryan, particularly of Bryan's preference for basing dollar value on the price of silver rather than the price of gold, as the Republicans supported. According to the *Cazenovia Republican*, Roosevelt's voice was hoarse, and he spoke "slowly and with evident effort," although his speech was clearly audible to everyone in the crowd. Roosevelt said he was especially happy to be in Cazenovia because it was the home of former Secretary of the Treasury Charles S. Fairchild, who, although a Democrat who served under Democrat President Grover Cleveland, was supporting the 1900 Republican ticket because of the silver versus gold monetary policy issue.

After Roosevelt's remarks, as the train pulled out of the station, "there was a great rush to grasp the governor's hand, and he stood stooping at the rear of the platform shaking hands with the people until the increasing speed of the train made it impossible to follow him," according to the *Cazenovia Republican.* "Yesterday was decidedly Roosevelt day in Cazenovia. His coming was the all-absorbing topic of the day's conversation, and but little business was transacted until after the special train had passed."

While Roosevelt did not stay long in Cazenovia in 1900, local lore states that he visited the village multiple times in later years, staying at Notleymere, the East Lake Road home of his friend Frank Norton. No historical evidence has been found to support this local legend, however, according to Russell Grills, Cazenovia historian and author of the books *Upland Idyll: Images of Cazenovia, New York, 1860–1900* and *Cazenovia: The Story of an Upland Community.*

Unlike Grover Cleveland, Theodore Roosevelt was not president of the United States when he visited Cazenovia, although he was governor of the state. It was only eleven months after his visit, however, that President McKinley was shot by anarchist Leon Czolgosz at the Pan American Exposition in Buffalo on September 6, 1901. McKinley died eight days later, on September 14, after which Roosevelt was sworn in as the twenty-sixth president of the United States.

At the time President McKinley was shot, Vice President Roosevelt was at a luncheon at the Vermont Fish and Game League on Lake Champlain. He immediately traveled to Buffalo to be with the injured president. After a few days, McKinley's doctors assured everyone that the president was improving every day and would survive, so Roosevelt traveled to the Adirondacks to join his family on vacation there. According to historian Edmund Morris, Roosevelt's leave-taking from Buffalo was done to reassure the public that the president was recovering. Just days later, as Roosevelt and his family were hiking up Mount Marcy, the tallest mountain in New York state, a man arrived bearing a telegram for the vice president saying the president's condition was failing. After a second telegram was received saying that the president was dying, Roosevelt immediately set out for the nearest train station so he could get to Buffalo as soon as possible.

Roosevelt's subsequent thirty-five-mile journey down Mount Marcy in a buckboard in the dead of night has since become the stuff of legend.

He left his camp just before midnight for a ride that would take at least seven hours during the day. The trip over winding and rain-slick roads took three changes of wagons, with fresh horses and drivers each time, and lasted about six hours. According to one account, during the last leg of the journey, Mike Cronin, proprietor of Aiden Lair and Roosevelt's third driver that night, covered the sixteen-mile distance of winding mountain road in an hour and forty-one minutes, with Roosevelt himself holding the lantern in an attempt to light the road. According to writer Joan F. Aldous, Cronin stated that "Mr. Roosevelt was one of the nerviest men he ever saw" and that when he slowed the team in a dangerous place, Roosevelt responded, "If you are not afraid, I am not. Push ahead!"

When Roosevelt arrived at the North Creek train station at around 6 a.m. on the morning of September 14, his secretary was waiting for him with a telegram stating that the president had died.

A Family of Patriots

The Kent Brothers and Their World War I Service

The small village of Cazenovia is understandably proud of its native sons and daughters, many of whom have achieved national and international fame as educators, politicians, military heroes, and the occasional circus performer. Frequently lost among the list of prominent citizens, however, are the Kent brothers, who may have been the greatest concentration of talent an era had to offer. The Kent brothers are best known today for contributing four men from one family to serve in World War I, more than any other family in Madison County. And while their contributions to the war effort were honorable and impressive, it was their civilian achievements that have left indelible marks on our nation. The six (total) brothers each won acclaim, some on the national stage, in the fields of engineering, physics, and conservation, among others. They brought their impressive skills to bear in the service of their nation both in and out of uniform, and it was in Cazenovia that each began his journey to success.

The lineage of the Kent family, hailing from Meriden, Connecticut, can be traced to the pilgrims of the Mayflower, through the family's matriarch, Mary Chapman Kent. She was a descendant of both Deacon Denham of Plymouth and Thomas Olney, who settled Rhode Island with Roger Williams. Born in 1850, Mary received her college education at Falley Seminary in Fulton, New York. It was here where she met Silas Kent, whom she would marry soon after graduation. Her own foundational educational experience seems to have influenced her choices for her sons, whom she would guide into the halls of America's greatest educational institutions.

Silas and Mary's second son, William, left for Cazenovia to attend the renowned seminary there in 1897. The Kents decided to relocate the family

THREE BROTHERS FROM CAZENOVIA IN THE SERVICE

CAPT. ROBERT H. KENT
Cazenovia, N. Y.

ENSIGN S. S. KENT
Cazenovia, N. Y.

LIEUT. CHESTER B. KENT
Cazenovia, N. Y.

28. Robert, Stanley, and Chester Kent, three of the four Kent brothers who served in World War I and would go on to acclaim in a variety of fields. Courtesy of the New York State Archives.

to the village the next year, in 1898, settling on upper Lincklaen Street. The Cazenovia Seminary would prove to be the launching pad that set five of the brothers on their future paths. William, Edwin, Robert, Silas, and Olney would all attend in turn. Only the eldest, Chester, would miss the opportunity. Following the seminary, the brothers completed their educations at some of the nation's foremost institutions, including four in the Ivy League. By the time the United States entered World War I in 1917, each of the brothers was already making a name for himself. But despite successful careers, Chester, Silas, William, and Robert would all come to the aid of their country, bringing along a startling variety of talent.

Chester C., the eldest son, born in 1874, had already served his country once, during the Spanish American War. He had operated as an officer in the signal corps, the Army's precursor to the intelligence and communication fields. After the conflict, he attended Wesleyan University and Syracuse University's law school. Upon graduation, he opened a law firm in the Rouse block of Cazenovia's thriving business district. His reputation in the village was so well respected that he was elected a justice of the peace as well as a member of the town board in the early years of the twentieth century. In 1913, Chester's three-year-old daughter Margaret passed away from diabetic coma and, one week later, the family patriarch, Silas William, would join her, leaving Chester as head of the Kent family.

At the declaration of war in 1917, Chester left his law firm in the hands of a partner and joined the Army's field artillery service as an orientation officer. Lieutenant Kent, stationed in England, was responsible for making maps directing the trajectory of field artillery. A talent with ordnance trajectory may have run in the family, because Chester's famous younger brother, Robert, would become an innovator in a similar field. Upon his return to the United States in 1919, Chester took up the reins of law in Cazenovia once more. His ties to the village were strong, but when he was elected a trustee of the New York National Bank in 1922 he chose to move his family to Albany. He continued there in the state income tax department until his sudden death of a heart attack in 1950. Of the Kent brood, Chester remained the closest to Cazenovia, returning frequently to visit his widowed mother until her death.

Certainly, the most colorful of the brothers was William H. B. Kent. Born in 1878, it was his attendance at the Cazenovia Seminary which brought his family to the village. His mark, however, would be made out west in America's national parks and in the country's collective imagining of the Old West. After studying forestry management at Syracuse University, William joined the US Forestry Service and decamped for the Pacific Northwest, where his detailed reports of the Cascades, Yellowstone National Park, and areas of the southwest would eventually help preserve some of our national treasures. Known to his companions in the Forestry Service as "Whiskey High Balls" Kent for his penchant for strong drink, he was considered "a maverick ranger, wearing a bandana instead of the regulation Stetson," and reciting poetry at his meetings. His greatest achievement as a conservationist came in 1910 when he spent a week detailing undeveloped wilderness tracts in telegrams to Washington, DC. His painstaking reports helped President William Howard Taft expand national park lands ahead of a congressional deadline. For his conservation efforts, Kent is memorialized at Kent Springs in the Santa Rita mountains of Arizona.

After his work in the west, William sailed to the Philippine Islands to detail natural resources there. He contracted malaria and left the Forestry

Service soon after. William returned home to Cazenovia to recover and raised chickens on a farm on Lincklaen Street, presumably to contribute to the family coffers. When America entered World War I, William chose to enlist, bringing his mapmaking and scouting skills to the Army's intelligence department. He arrived in France in September 1918 and was quickly advanced to participate in the battle of Argonne Forest, the final—and largest—battle in World War I. When he returned to the United States, William moved west once again to Glendora, California, this time to write Western novels about the land he so dearly loved. Two of his short stories, "Tenderfoot" and "Range Rider," were published in the 1940s and are still available for purchase today. The stories centered on a lone cowboy, battling for justice in the untamed expanse of Arizona. It was a theme that would explode in popularity in the post–World War II years. Unfortunately, William would not live to see it. He passed away in 1947 at his home in California, one year after the publication of "Range Rider" and just before the publication of "Tenderfoot."

Two of the six Kent brothers did not serve in World War I: Dr. Edwin, a medical missionary to China, and Dr. Olney, a professor at Cornell University. Edwin, born in 1882, attended Cazenovia Seminary followed by Boston University. His family's strong ties to the Methodist Episcopal church led him to serve as superintendent of the Methodist hospital in Changli, China, in the early 1900s. He returned home in 1915 due to an unspecified illness and his family settled in the Adirondacks in hopes of effecting a recovery. When his condition worsened once again, they moved to Cazenovia, where Edwin passed away among family in 1917. The youngest son, Olney, born in 1890, had been the salutatorian of his 1909 graduating class at the Cazenovia Seminary before completing his education at Cornell University. He was the second person in the country to be awarded a doctorate in poultry studies and was offered the position of professor of animal husbandry at the institution shortly after. During World War I, he served his country on the home front, "actively engaged in agricultural work," (as the *Cazenovia Republican* newspaper put it) as the assistant farm bureau manager for Oswego County—a post no less important, if less glamorous, than that of his brothers. In the 1920s Olney's scientific skills were scouted by the Quaker Oats Company, and he relocated to Libertyville, Illinois, where he led the company's research farm, becoming a leader in agricultural science. Olney passed away at the age of sixty-six at his vacation home in Switzerland, leaving a legacy in research and innovation in the food sciences.

Silas, who frequently went by "Stanley," the youngest brother but one, was the only Kent brother to earn a decoration during World War I. Born in 1887, Silas attended the Cazenovia Union school and seminary in the family tradition. He followed up his education at Harvard engineering school, earning his degree in civil engineering. When war was declared, Silas was working for the Massachusetts Commission on Waterways and Public Lands, but he chose to enlist in the Naval Reserve and was assigned to officer training. He would eventually oversee the construction of U-boat-chasing vessels, one of the innovations of the Great War. He then stepped into the role of commander, as Ensign Kent, aboard U-Boat Chaser 260, a 110-foot-long, twenty-man submarine chaser that patrolled the English Channel for German U-boats. His vessel's purpose was to locate the U-boats using hydrophone listening devices and then destroy them with depth-charged bombs. The boats were an entirely new form of naval offense, meant to strike back at Germany's unrestricted submarine warfare. That Silas was placed in a position to oversee their production as well as the command of his own vessel bespeaks the depth of his engineering knowledge. He was awarded the Navy Cross for his service in a sea engagement during the summer of 1918.

Unruffled by the drama of naval warfare, Silas wrote home that "it is all very interesting, and I enjoy it immensely." He seemed grateful for the chance to see the world, calling it compensation for the hard work his crew performed. America's U-boat chasers reportedly sank over twenty German U-boats and damaged many more, helping to sustain the Allied blockade of the Central Powers. In the spring of 1919, Silas was transferred to the USS *Piqua*, a patrol vessel, acting as engineering officer, and later, navigating officer. When he returned to the United States that summer, he hastened back to Lowell, Massachusetts, where he was hired as chief engineer by the Canals and Locks Association. There he would build and maintain the waterways surrounding the area, protecting the viaducts for commercial use. He remained in the area until his death in 1943.

In an extraordinarily talented family, one brother stands out for his groundbreaking innovations and achievements, as well as for his service during World War I. Robert H. Kent, fourth of the six brothers, has been called the chief US expert in ballistics, father of modern military ordnance, and one of our country's most exceptional mathematical minds. His achievements in the fields of ballistics, physics, and engineering comprise a laundry list of awards, directorships, and inventions. But of course, it all began in Cazenovia.

Like his brothers, he attended the Cazenovia Seminary before heading off to the halls of the Ivy League. By the time he left for college, Robert's acumen with numbers was already well established. He won the seminary's achievement prize in trigonometry at graduation in 1906. A note in the *Cazenovia Republican*'s annual list of distinguished scholars says: "A perusal of the above shows how good scholarship often runs in families. Note the frequent occurrence of the names Andrews and Kent." The Kent brothers had a peerless reputation for academic success at the seminary, a reputation they maintained throughout their lives.

Silas and Mary Kent had hopes that Robert would carry on the family's Methodist tradition and sent him to Columbia College for training as a preacher. Robert had his own ideas, however, and left Columbia soon after. He transferred to the physics program at Harvard, where he studied mathematics and theoretical physics and ballistics, the computation of guiding explosives on their intended path. After graduation, Robert served as an assistant professor of physics and an instructor of mathematics at the school while he wrote his doctoral thesis on the theoretical physics of intermolecular repulsion. At the time, Harvard considered physics strictly an experimental science and declined to grant him a doctorate. Robert refused to compromise his thesis to suit the school's definitions and would continue his career without his doctoral degree until 1953 when Harvard awarded him the honorary degree of Doctor of Science.

In 1917, Robert joined the Army, leaving his post as professor of electrical engineering at the University of Pennsylvania. He initially volunteered as a pilot with the Aviation Branch and was "tremendously relieved when the officer told me I was four months too old to be an aviator," he wrote. He next offered his services to the Coast Artillery Corps when he was recruited by an ordnance officer shortly thereafter. With characteristic humor, Robert recounts that his coastal commander advised him to take the ordnance position because, "In my opinion, you're not a very military person." Robert took this advice and was commissioned a first lieutenant.

Soon after, Robert traveled to Tours, France, where he served on the staff of the chief ordnance officer as an expert ballistician, creating field maps and determining the trajectory of shells and the explosives required to reach their target. The field was relatively new and changing rapidly with the development of guns like the eight-inch Howitzer and Germany's long-range Paris Gun. Robert developed firing tables that computed the correct angles and ranges for each missile. The field commanders relied heavily on the accuracy of the tables for Allied defenses. Robert also served as American representative at various firing tests and demonstrations. It was during these assignments that he formed associations with other innovative scientists like Sir Ralph Fowler and Sir Alwyn Crow of Britain. These connections would last a lifetime, and through them Robert would collaborate on some of his grandest innovations.

Although Robert retired from the Army two years later, his career with the US military was far from over. The government was so impressed by his knowledge of ballistics that he was asked to join the Office of the Chief of Ordnance and, later, moved to the Aberdeen Proving Ground in Maryland, the Army's premier ordnance research and testing facility. There he would develop and test theories regarding rocket flight and missile guidance systems that would be integral to the military's rapidly developing arsenal during World War II and the Cold War. He served as chairman of the Explosives and Armament Panel of the Air Force Scientific Advisory Board as well as a member of the National Academy of Sciences and as a fellow of the American Physical Society. "Kent's powers were multiplied many times by his ability to work through others," fellow scientist Leslie E. Simon said, "and the people who are indebted to Kent are legion." His work would inspire a future generation of researchers and help make America's armed forces second to none.

Robert continued to live and work in Havre de Grace, Maryland, close to the Aberdeen Proving Ground, until his death in 1961 at the age of seventy-five. He was the last of the six Kent brothers and was survived by his three nephews and three nieces. His life was remembered by colleagues and friends as one not only of extraordinary achievement but also kindness and warmth. His disposition was such that "Without any known exception, every man who knew Kent liked him; most loved him," colleagues said.

During his life, Robert would return to Cazenovia occasionally to visit his mother and eventually brought her to live with him in Maryland. Mary Kent returned to Cazenovia every summer, living in the family home on Lincklaen Street until her death in 1941 at the age of ninety-one. The Kent family were famous in their time for their patriotism in lending the services of four brave brothers during the Great War. Their contributions during a time of national need were significant, with each brother serving with honor and distinction. However, it was the Kent brothers' contributions away from the front lines which are truly remarkable. The mark of Mary and Silas Kent's six sons can be seen one hundred years on through their work in the fields of science, conservation, and engineering, among others. Today, Cazenovia may remember the boys, but the nation remembers the men.

"Nothing Further Remains but Our Duty"

Cecil Donovan's Letters from the Western Front

The young men of Cazenovia were quick to answer their nation's call when the United States entered World War I in 1917. Cecil Vincent Donovan was one of nearly two hundred young Cazenovians to serve his country during the conflict and one of only two awarded the Croix de Guerre, France's highest honor for bravery in service. But Cecil served his community in a more direct way as well. His frequent letters home, published in the *Cazenovia Republican*, described both the horrors and surprising humor of life on the Western Front.[1] Donovan's letters gave his community a personal glimpse into the war that news reports could not, or would not, provide. His letters detailed the boredom, fear, and heroism that readers' relatives and friends were facing and helped give them a better understanding of the sacrifices their countrymen were making in Europe.

Born in 1897, Cecil was the only son of William T. and Florence Donovan. William was a successful monument maker and served as a village trustee and leader in the Methodist church. Cecil enjoyed a typical village upbringing with an education at the Cazenovia Union School followed by the Cazenovia Seminary. He demonstrated an aptitude for art early in life and upon graduation from the Seminary continued his studies at Syracuse

---

1. Cecil Donovan's annotated letters used for this chapter were retrieved from the archives of the *Cazenovia Republican*. Donovan's letters are not otherwise available in any archive or museum as far as has been discovered. A more thorough compendium of his communications may reside with his descendants.

University's Crouse Fine Arts School. Cecil had recently held his first art exhibition on the university campus when the United States entered World War I in April of 1917. In response to the nation's call to arms, he and twenty-one other university students formed the Syracuse University Ambulance Unit and departed for France in August. There, they were trained to perform the dangerous task of transporting wounded soldiers from the front lines of the war to field hospitals at the rear. As though the task were not daunting enough, rattletrap ambulances struggling through knee-deep mud soon became targets of German bombing raids. During the winter of 1917–18, Cecil and nine other men from his unit were awarded the Croix du Guerre by the French government for their meritorious service in action. He was the first Cazenovian decorated in the conflict, and one of only two from the local area to receive the award.

Aside from his vivid descriptions of the war, a running theme in Donovan's letters is his attempt to capture the scenery and human experiences around him through his sketches and photographs. His artistic expertise must have been considerable because in December of 1917 his sketches were requested by Major Andrews of the US Army as a contribution to the American Field Service commemorative book. Cecil writes that he "would like to keep my sketches for myself but I suppose it would be rather good to have them printed in this book," which it seems he did. Despite his hesitance to publish his pictures at that time, his war experiences would inspire many of his most influential later works, such as a watercolor piece titled "Retreat," which juxtaposed the silhouettes of soldiers against the shadows of the French countryside.

Donovan's first letters, written on the transport ship to France, arrived home in September, nearly a month after he departed. They reflected a hunger for adventure and an excitement to join the big parade. "This is surely the most wonderful trip I have ever made," he wrote in August of 1917, "The peril of the submarine adds to the voyage, that delicious tinge of danger and thrill which make it quite complete."

Here are excerpts from some of his letters home:

Friday, August 17, 1917

I little thought one year ago now, when I was working in the canning factory, that I would be having this kind of a vacation. This is surely the most wonderful trip I have ever made. The peril of the submarine adds to the voyage, that delicious tinge of danger and thrill which make it quite complete. The sea is rather rough to-night and a good many of the fellows are seasick. So far I am feeling fine, except for the first two days out, when I had a bad headache but am feeling like a king now.

It is getting rather monotonous by now, the same thing day after day. Just lay around and read, promenade, play shuffle board, etc. We have now about 5 or 6 more days before we land again. We land in Bordeaux and go from there to Paris by train. I hope we go in the daytime so it will be possible for us to enjoy the scenery.

The world is such a small place. I have met a Rev. Mr. Beekman who knows Cazenovia quite well. He and his wife are going over. Then another is Bishop Wilson of the M.E. church who is going over to inspect the Red Cross. The famous magazine writer, Stephen A. White, is on board and a very interesting man to talk with. A man named Mr. Moore who is to be head of the U.S. postal service in France with Pershing's forces is also quite a friend of mine by this time. He knows the Krumbhaar's of Cazenovia.

There are so many people here who amount to so much, and who are also so willing to talk with one that the hours go quickly by.

September 12, 1917

I saw a great sight yesterday afternoon while at the front. A German aeroplane and two French planes were having a fight, nearly overhead. I could hear their machine guns popping and suddenly the Boche plane was hit in the gas tank which exploded and set them on fire. They fell over and over all ablaze and landed very close to where I was stationed. I got permission and went over and took a picture of it. The two men in the plane were killed by the fall of course and then their bodies burned in the wreckage. An awful mess to see.

It's great out on the front nights to see the star shells go up and the signal lights. We have to eat and sleep in dugouts about 25 or 30 feet underground. The food here isn't as bad as it is in some places but if you want good meals my advice is to stay on your side of the Atlantic. Sometime when you haven't got anything to do just send me over a can or two of jam. We haven't any butter of course and without something it is almost impossible to eat the bread here. O'well as the French say "c'est le guerre," which means "it is the war."

October 5, 1917

We often make runs in this sector of 30 miles or more. As you say, I have some hardships, but while they may seem hard at the time, after they are over and done with, I laugh and don't let it worry me. Last night for instance was not so easy. This section has been taken over by new men and we are going to be sent somewhere else. I had one of these new men out with me at a front poste, and over a tortuous road that I had been over only once. In the middle of the night we had a blessé, and had to roll. The night was black as ink, and a heavy fog. The road was full of shell holes and very muddy. I let the new man drive, and he took a wrong road. Finally we ran into a lot of soft mud and stuff which was heaped up in the road. The car was absolutely stuck. The stuff heaped up over the front axle and the differential was sunk in also. We had to crawl under the car and dig it out with our hands. After a while I got the car out and drove back to the other road. We then got out to walk and look for the right turn. After we had gone a little distance the Boche began to throw in shells. We dropped flat in the mud and I rolled over in the ditch which was a little deeper, but it was also full of water. The shells blew about 200 feet off and threw dirt around and the éclat hit a horse in the road. In a minute we had time to hit the right road and get the car and get out of there. After a while we arrived and then I had a good thirteen hour sleep.

This morning my clothes were a sorry sight. But it is things like that all the time and the only way to do it is just make the best of it, and let it go at that.

The other night I went through the air in an auto smash up, for some distance, and landed on velvet. Of course I was lucky.

It is very difficult to send any photographs as the censors might stop them. But I will have a wonderful collection when I return. In my estimation they are a much better than a lot of shells and Boche helmets, etc.

Yes, war is all that Sherman said it was and some others around here put it much stronger and picturesquely. The food is not bad

always, and when we get under the American officers we will get
much better food. The English officers and men are all betting 10
to 1 that the war will be over in January. I would like to take some
of that money and I would even be glad to lose. I don't think that it
will be finished in January, but I do think that it will be over by next
November.

Yes, the scenery in New York State has got it over anything
where I am now. The Champagne district of France is flat, and the
soil is all chalk. The chalk makes the roads white, which is a help at
night.

Cecil Donovan

But as weeks turned into months and Cecil faced the horrors of trench
warfare, his tone began to change from eagerness to boredom and finally
disgust and dejection.

October 10, 1917

The other day I was at the "triage" poste, and a dead French-
man floated past in the river just back of us. At first we thought he
was a dead Boche, but on hauling him out we found that he was a
poiler, his head half shot off. This morning I arose at 6 o'clock, as
we had to evacuate two hospitals. Oh, if you could only see these
poor men! It wasn't the shells, it wasn't the battlefields that brought
war home to me, but the hospitals showed it to me. The rows and
rows of maimed and broken men. And they are brave, oh, so brave.
They carried a young chap into my car who had both eyes shot
out and had been horribly wounded. Still he joked with his comrades, and bade them a cheerful farewell. Practically all of them
are the same. It seems too hard, these many men in the prime of
life, and destined to go on till the end, dependent upon the help of
others. Perhaps I shouldn't write of these distressing things, but I
have been so impressed that I can't resist the temptation to tell you
about them.

The weather continues as usual, rain and more rain. Yesterday
afternoon I had to go to an artillery poste and drove through thin
mud nearly up to the axel. The only thing I was thankful for was
that I did not have a blowout or puncture.

Paris, December 22, 1917

Paris is very gay now at Christmas time and I am enjoying myself a great deal. If you think that things are dear in the States you should live over here for awhile. Everything is perfectly exorbitant.

There is lots of talk of a big Boche attack and when I go back I'll probably land in the thick of it.

It seems so strange to see on all the little French news stands, the Saturday Post prominently displayed.

The streets are just filled with men of all nations. In the theatre "Follies Bergere" one may see uniforms from all the countries of the allies. One hears almost as much English spoken in Paris as French.

I wish I could write a description of the boulevards and streets so that you might be able to see the color and the gaiety of the crowds. Yet underneath it all seems to be a suppressed sadness. There are more beautiful girls to the square inch in Paris than any other place in the world.

I received a letter from Major Andrews of the U.S. Army today asking me to donate some sketches to a large book which he is compiling of the American Field Service. I would like to keep my sketches for myself but I suppose it would be rather good to have them printed in this book.

Despite the mud, the cold, and the danger, Cecil and his comrades held fast to their natural exuberance. Their antics may have amused the locals, but they also helped keep the spark of hope and humanity alive in the soldiers.

January 11, 1918

This evening we had quite a time and amused the whole town who no doubt were saying to themselves, "Those crazy Americans." We have a small stream back of our cantonment which empties into the larger river--, which flows nearby. As the ice in the small stream was a little loose, we thought we could clear it all out. So we put on boots and went to it. We broke it into pieces and shoveled it out into the current. After a while we had a big piece and a fellow and I thought we would take a ride. So we jumped on and were off. We sailed along very nicely, regarding the city's beauty from a new angle. All was pretty as a wedding bell (or something like that) until we reached a jumping off place at a big water gate. Some women washing clothes in the river were sure we were going to destruction in the race way and ran screaming up and down the banks. Soon the shores were lined with people and we approached our end faster and faster. As we neared the high stone wall my partner jumped and kicked the end of ice away, so I had to jump, but I couldn't make the wall. He was still hanging on the edge but I grabbed his hand and there we hung. I'm sure Douglass Fairbanks couldn't have done better. We had the whole crowd breathing in gasps and mighty few clothes were washed for a while. We climbed up the wall made our bow and walked back to the cantonment. So far Eliza crossing the ice had nothing on us, but the old saw that "pride goeth before a fall" was right and we were due to get ours in short order.

Some arch fiend in human shape had another big piece of ice and suggested that four of us take another little ride. We felt pretty good and said, "Sure, let's go." Charlie Howard, the other fellow and myself mounted the old piece of ice, but our wise guy made some remark that perhaps four were too many and gave us a shove out into the current. Well, that was a mighty unstable foundation. First she began to sink and then she turned over. Sprague yells "every man for himself" and the splash he made was fine. Nothing else to do but swim and that was no cinch with rubber boots on but we made it to shore easily and did a quick change into dry clothes. The end of a perfect day. Anyway we entertained about 350 natives which wasn't bad. I'm in the best of health.

In the midst of winter in 1918, Cecil wrote: "I sincerely hope it will be the last one [winter] I have to spend over here. I don't know where we will stay for all the houses are destroyed." In Cecil's early letters, he described researching and visiting Parisian art schools in hopes of completing his undergraduate study in France. But as the war wore on, Cecil mentioned it less and less and eventually seems to have abandoned interest in the plan. Paris had lost its luster for the young artist. "Nothing further remains but our duty," he wrote in the spring of 1918, "and the sight of a beautiful town crumpling to pieces while we watch."

January 18, 1918

I had a funny experience myself the other night. I had to carry a couple of men up to the front. Passed one of our cars in the ditch. The roads were covered with ice. As we are not allowed to use chains, I slid all over the road, got shoved up a hill by a regiment or so of men, and finally arrived. Coming back I had to drive through a town that in pre-war years was a beautiful peaceful retreat for artists, and the scene of gay hunting parties, but is now nothing but ruins. Picture a night like Calvary. Dark heavy clouds hanging low and a streak angry sunset. I came slowly down the road from under the shelter of the hill.

Just before I turned the corner into the village, Crash! And behind a house in front of me a shell blew. Well, I didn't hesitate very long there. But as I went up the road six more landed back there. The funny part was that just as one went off I hit my head on the small window back of me which had come open. I thought I was surely dead then.

In one poignant letter from 1918, Cecil expressed his pleasure at meeting Ms. Marion Crandell, one of the Americans providing a precious respite for soldiers in the form of the YMCA's Foyer du Soldat, or "Soldier's Fireside." Marion was a well-educated teacher from Iowa who had resigned her position in order to serve her country overseas. She and Cecil were both stationed in St. Menehould, near the front lines, though Cecil was not allowed to mention his location in his letters. He recounted his last meeting with her in May of that year, the day before she was killed by a German bomb. She and Cecil seemed to have shared a love of culture and the arts and he mentioned she was arranging for a concert to entertain the men. Cecil's description of her death is heavy with a weariness and resignation about the war. "We all felt terribly about it," he wrote. "She was buried with military honors in the huge cemetery outside the town where lie thousands of soldiers." She would be the first American woman in active service killed in the conflict. "I have given up all hopes of the war ending soon," he wrote while on leave (en permission) in Paris, "and am quite resigned to my fate. The general opinion in Paris is that it will last for anywhere from 3 to 15 years more. I wouldn't be surprised." Shortly thereafter Cecil's unit would be involved in the battles of the Spring Offensive where his bravery and endurance would earn him the Croix de Guerre, the highest honor bestowed by the French government.

May 2, 1918

I am now in the South of dear old France, en permission, and, believe me, I was glad to come here. For the past few weeks I have been in hell, and that is not profanity but a simple interpretation of my life for the short time past. How thankful I am, that you in the United States, do not know what really happens over here. Of course you read in the papers, so many men killed, but it is impossible for you to realize what this means. You can't visualize the suffering, silent suffering and the tragedy of it all, and for that I am glad. May it always be that you will never know the pain of being driven from your peaceful home, driven out into the rain and cold, forced to walk miles under conditions impossible to tell about, forced to degradations that cause one to shudder. All these things I have seen, and I assure you that the picture is not a pleasant one.

Two of our boys are now resting under the sod and two others in the hospital may be counted among the casualties any time. Oh, the life I've recently lived! Although it is a few days behind me and in the past, it has so seared itself into my brain that although I live to be a thousand, I can never forget. You, living in your peaceful home, can never know what it means to have death suddenly fall upon you. One deafening crash and then the sickening moan of dear ones who are wounded even unto death. Each night I pray that it may all end soon. It doesn't seem possible that I can go on with such an existence for long. The nights on the road, dark as Cavalry, and the skeleton of death lurking always before, behind and about one. It is granted to but few of this world to see a glimpse of the eternal life and return to the petty cares and tasks of this life. Perhaps I should not tell you all this, but my heart is overflowing with what I have been through there in the North.

During the last crises when the grey hordes of the Hun came pouring in overwhelming numbers upon the British and our brave poilus, all permissions were stopped. We worked day and night, with no sleep, little to eat and cared for neither. The air was full of electricity, everyone was keyed up until it seemed that soon something would snap in the brain. I have never endured such headache, and yet it didn't bother me, almost I seemed another person, and the one who suffered was not I. Blessed occurrence, there came a lull and one of our section was allowed to go en permission, and still luckier chance, that one was I. Oh, the relief to sleep and sleep and sleep. The sleep in a bed with sheets and have no fear of a sudden death, and yet, even now, I start up in my sleep and it is a second or so before I can realize where I am. No permission ever seemed so welcome as this one. I can't describe the place to you adequately now, but can only say that it is beautiful in the fullest measure of that word.

I have no idea where my section is now. En repos somewhere I suppose. I have met some very interesting people down here. A Mr. and Mrs. Corry, who are Irish, but have lived abroad for a great number of years. They know a number of great people in Germany, princes, etc., and know about conditions there. Last Sunday afternoon I had tea with them at their villa, a most beautiful place, by the way, and I learned many interesting things. They were great friends of J. P. Morgan, who used to come here quite a bit.

We had news in our section before I came away, that we were to be cited for the French war cross, for our work in the great attack. When I learn more about it, I will tell you. We did nothing remarkably brave except carrying [the censor has here with scissors cut out the next word which probably was a number] men in one night and a day under continual shell fire. One night we had eight cars smashed, but otherwise we came out fortunately, with the exception of two boys in the hospital.

But of course, with the signing of the Armistice on November 11th of 1918, the war eventually limped to a close. The villagers of Cazenovia celebrated with pealing bells and a boisterous parade through the streets. Now began the task of demobilizing and reuniting young men with their families. When Donovan returned home in the spring of 1919, he recommenced his artistic studies at Syracuse University, eventually graduating with a Master of Fine Arts from Crouse College. His talent as an abstractionist, honed by his time overseas and diligent study, would gain him fame in the coming decades. He became a professor of art at the University of Illinois, where it was said he taught nearly every art class available for study. During his tenure, he helped found the internationally renowned Krannert Art Museum and served as its director until his retirement in 1965. He would continue to exhibit his art in studios throughout the country, including Central New York, for many years to come. Many of his pieces featured scenes from war-torn France as well as of his beloved Cazenovia, where he and his family would summer for many years. He and his wife Blanche retired to Santa Barbara, California in the 1960s where he would remain until his death in 1987.

One hundred years on, Cecil's letters remain as vivid and compelling as when they were first published. His language with its use of slang terms and his unsparing descriptions of violence have a particularly modern tone. And as a primary resource, the letters are invaluable for their depictions of the famous, the infamous, and especially the nameless actors on the world's stage. Thanks to the *Cazenovia Republican*'s support of its sons in arms, modern historians and readers alike may reap the benefits of historic hindsight through one courageous artist's eyes.

A Colorful Cazenovia Character

Circus Man Jim Fitch

In Cazenovia's 225-year history, many fascinating people have called the community home. One of the most colorful characters to have ever lived here was undoubtedly Jim Fitch—a world-traveled circus performer, town steeplejack, and trainer of squirrels. Photos of Jim doing the "double hand horizontal" handstand and headstands on the Cazenovia Presbyterian Church steeple in 1921 have been published in the *Cazenovia Republican* at least a half-dozen times, while Jim's history, hijinks, and daily activities have been the subject of newspaper stories more than fifty times over a seventy-five-year period.

According to published sources and personal reminiscences, Jim was fun, exciting, kind, and quirky. "Everybody knows Jim, nobody hates him, and the whole town is proud of him," as one townsman wrote in 1942. Yet simultaneously, Jim was apparently an alcoholic and somewhat of a vagrant who would often get himself arrested in winter so he would have a warm place to sleep on cold nights. Similar to another famous Cazenovian, Lucy "Crazy Luce" Dutton, Fitch's duality of character makes it certain that the pleasant wonder of his memory may not be as accurately human as his true story.

Fitch was born in Cazenovia in 1874, the son of Derek Fitch, an accomplished engineer, inventor, and cofounder of what would become the Cazenovia Telephone Company. Jim's mother, Mary (Haws), was described as a "fine woman of strong character," who bore four children, of which Jim was the youngest. Jim apparently helped his father often in the electronics and telephone businesses, but then ran away from home at age fifteen and joined the circus—a career that would span thirty years and allow him

29 & 30. These two 1921 photos showcase acrobat Jim Fitch and the talent that made him a local legend, as he performs acrobatic tricks atop the First Presbyterian Church steeple in Cazenovia. Courtesy Chris and Judi Randall and Cazenovia Public Library.

to travel throughout the country and the world with some of the greatest, most popular shows of the era.

When Jim left Cazenovia in about 1889 to join the circus, he started with Charles Lee's Great London Circus doing a tumbling act. Through the years, he learned magic tricks, wire walking, bareback riding, tumbling, animal training, and husbandry, but his specialty was on the flying trapeze as an "aerialist," according to his friend William O. Aikman, who wrote an article titled "Everybody Knows Jim" in 1942. *Cazenovia Republican* editor J. C. Peck, who was a close friend to Fitch, said Jim could do "almost anything around a circus" and was "one of the best in the business."

In addition to Lee's Great London Circus, Fitch was with the Walter L. Main three-ring circus, the Sig Sautelle Circus, and spent two summers touring the western United States with the Sells-Floto Circus. While with

Sells-Floto, he secured a job for fellow Cazenovian Zora Card, who later became internationally famous as "Mademoiselle Zora," the tiger and elephant tamer. Fitch also spent seven winters playing the B. F. Keith Circuit in vaudeville, touring the United States and Canada. The Cazenovia-born aerialist also worked the bigger circus outfits in his career, including Cole Brothers, Barnum and Bailey's (in India, he once said), and Buffalo Bill's Wild West Show. Fitch spent two years with Buffalo Bill as the show toured Europe, playing in London, Paris, Berlin, and most of the large cities. According to a 1941 article in the *Cazenovia Republican*, Fitch was the top man on a four-man-high tumbling team in Buffalo Bill's show. "Standing on each other's shoulders Jim was the top or fourth man of the pyramid and way up there in the stratosphere he did his stuff, somersaults, etc."

While working in the Wild West Show, Fitch met Billy Nichols, with whom he worked and remained friends for years. The two originated the "Japanese Break-Away Ladder Act," also called the "Japanese Ladder Trick," in which Nichols would balance a forty-foot ladder on his shoulders and Fitch would climb to the top and do his tricks. At a signal—usually a loud report, as from a gun—the ladder would come apart, leaving Fitch standing on the top on just one upright, according to Aikman. According to Fitch's friend Walter G. Chard, Jim was the first "white man" to do the Japanese break-away ladder trick, and he was the top man because he was so light. "Jim went around the world with Buffalo Bill's Wild West Show," Chard wrote in 1950. "He told me many interesting details of Buffalo Bill's life and the girls who traveled with the show." In 1896, Charles Lee's Great London Circus advertised "Nichols and Fitch, Japanese perch and double trapeze" as performers, while the duo also performed the act together in August 1900 at the Morrisville Firemen's Inspection Day event.

Aikman recalled that whenever Fitch would return to Cazenovia to visit, he would often bring Nichols with him and the two would give a performance and "pass the hat" for money. The pair also once performed their trapeze act without a net on Albany Street, swinging thirty feet in the air from arms attached to the Republican and Democratic flag poles in the middle of the village.

"Several Cazenovians remember when they were boys watching 'Fitch & Nichols' practicing their act in a vacant lot on the east side of Farnham Street," according to the *Cazenovia Republican* in 1941. "Nichols balanced the pole on his shoulder without touching his hands to it while Jim high up the pole did unbelievable stunts. The act broke up when Jim and Will each got sweet on the same circus lady and Jim atop the pole began to wonder if he could still trust Nichols." Aikman also states that the acrobatic pair dissolved their partnership because of an amorous rivalry. Fitch stayed in the circus for a few more years after that, but then came home to Cazenovia to settle down.

In November 1904, Fitch, a thirty-one-year-old painter, married Edyth J. Stearns, age twenty-eight, in a ceremony in the Cazenovia Presbyterian church. Stearns was the daughter of John H. and Hattie L. (Soule) Stearns and, according to a newspaper article, attended Henley Shorthand College in Syracuse in the years prior to her marriage. At some point, the marriage apparently ended, and Mrs. Fitch was living in California by 1917 and in Indiana in 1947. The only existing record of what happened to the couple comes from Aikman's 1942 article, in which he stated that Jim was a miserable husband because of his shrewish mother-in-law, who lived with the couple. His misery drove him to drink, and he spent more and more time in bars until his wife divorced him. Jim went back to the circus after that, until his retirement from the sawdust ring in about 1921, when he came back permanently to Cazenovia.

In Cazenovia, Fitch was a colorful character known and remembered for numerous reasons. He was a jack-of-all-trades who would do almost any job he could find: shovel walkways in winter and sweep sidewalks in summer; paint poles, steeples, houses, and boats; or clean a well, cellar, or rugs. Many people remembered him as an avid mushroomer—as well as an avid drinker. His main occupation was as the town steeplejack—a person who climbs tall structures such as chimneys and steeples in order to carry out repairs or painting. Many of the mentions of Jim Fitch that can be found in the *Cazenovia Republican* archives are small notices about him painting flagpoles, water towers, and church steeples in Cazenovia and surrounding communities, throughout New York State, and even in Ohio and Pennsylvania.

He apparently never had a regular address but would sleep sometimes in the old livery stable or in an abandoned house by the railroad tracks. According to Aikman, Fitch also had his "office" in a small courtyard between the hardware store warehouse and the old livery stable where he had gathered some old furniture and would spend his free time while doing his laundry in an old washtub. In winter, Fitch would harass or otherwise convince the county sheriffs to arrest him so he would have a warm place to sleep during cold weather.

Rocepha Lee remembered Fitch and the mushrooms he grew. "He spent the winters in the jail at Wampsville because it was warm," she told the local newspaper in 1977. Helen Kennard said the same, also in 1977, and recalled one winter when Fitch decided not to stay in the jail and instead took a job shoveling snow in the village. "One cold morning he made it all the way to Willowbank, the Kennard home, and announced, 'I shoveled a pint this morning,'" according to Kennard.

Theckla Constable Ledyard also remembered Fitch as an avid mushroomer who was "known to take a drink or two." She told the *Cazenovia Republican*: "One spring day Grandpa Ledyard was having a milk punch on the patio of Dr. Joy's house, across from Lorenzo. As the two old gents were sitting there, around the corner of the house came Jim Fitch on a mushroom foray. Dr. Joy looked at Jim and decided he needed a drink and offered him a milk punch. Jim didn't look too enthusiastic, but accepted and took a sip, whereupon the drink disappeared rapidly, followed by Jim's comment, 'My god what a cow!'"

Camilla (Davis) Viall remembered Fitch as being a fascinating character to the children of the village. "He loved kids; he'd greet you and all of sudden a nickel come out of your ear. Or he'd have a deck of cards, you'd pick one and put it back and he'd find it," she recalled. "He just was a really super nice guy. He did an awful lot around the village. In summer you could count on seeing him on the street—he just kind of was a fixture." Viall remembered kids often sitting in a circle around Fitch in the summertime, listening to him tell stories from his life. "If we saw that circle forming, we would run and sit in it," she said. "I suppose people nowadays would have thought that he was kind of a bum—not sure what they would call him today, roustabout, although we don't use that word anymore either."

William Dommett remembered being a child walking down the street with his mother when Fitch would stop and ask Dommett's mother for a quarter. "Then he would pull it out of my ear a few times and then, all of a sudden, he would not be able to find it again. He would say sorry to mom and I and go on off down the street looking for the next kid to try the same thing," Dommett said. "All the parents knew him and expected these little shows in the summertime." William G. Chard remembered Fitch doing the opposite—heading off for a drink with a quarter some friend had given him and, on the way to the bar, see poor kids looking wistfully in a candy store window. He would stop and talk to them, go inside, and come out with ice cream for them. "He did not get his drink— that was Jim," Chard told the newspaper in 1950.

Red Sanford recalled Fitch was also "a great character" and used to do cartwheels down the street.

C. Walter Driscoll remembered Fitch as being not only a circus performer and steeplejack, but also the local pool shark that could be found in Harry Rogers's pool room. "Many the traveling drummer who lost his week's commissions to that innocent appearing small-towner," Driscoll wrote.

Fitch also was well known then—and remembered later—for the tattoos that covered his body. In many of the reminiscences about him, the fact of his tattoos is mentioned. Fitch's friend Walter G. Chard, an avid amateur photographer, said he always wanted to photograph the tattoos on Jim's torso, but they never actually got around to doing it. Viall remembered that when it was hot in summer Fitch would have his shirt unbuttoned or completely off, and she could see the tattoos covering his chest and both arms. "Being a kid, it just fascinated me that he had all this color on him," she said. Lula L. Moon recalled of Fitch, "His firm, smooth chest was bared, that we, a tattooed sailor, all might see. 'You like it, hey?' he'd ask . . . got that down south, back when I was a boy—and look at this!' He'd roll his shirt sleeve high. 'My dancing doll, tattooed upon this muscle here.' He made her dance, as he would lightly hum a tune."

Fitch was famous inside and outside Cazenovia for another unique trait—his penchant for training squirrels. In March 1921, the fact that he trained a red squirrel was reported in Cazenovia and then picked up by the Empire State News Exchange and printed in papers throughout the state. According to the story, Fitch started taming the squirrel in summer 1920 when it was young, "until now it wears a collar and leash, shakes hands and will play dead." When the squirrel would tire of doing tricks it would jump into Fitch's coat pocket, out of sight. According to the article, Fitch and his aunt, Charlotte Haws, had trained a squirrel in a similar manner "some years ago."

In January 1923, Fitch again made the papers with the news that he was training a new red squirrel, after his previous one had been killed by a cat. His new friend had been pushed out of its nest by its mother, and Fitch rescued it and began feeding it with a medicine dropper. "Although it is only five weeks old it already can shake hands and do a few other simple tricks," according to the *Cazenovia Republican*. "If it squeals at night Jim gets up and warms milk for it. He carries the squirrel in his pocket."

That squirrel, named Dickey, had "quite a repertoire of tricks," but in October 1923 it escaped under the porch of Dr. Ellsworth Eliot's summer home at the head of Sullivan Street. Despite Fitch's numerous attempts to regain his pet using different types of animal traps, Dickey outsmarted him every time, according to the newspaper. "Jim says he will catch him in the end with patience of which he seems to have an unlimited supply," according to the article. By January 1924, Fitch had begun training his third squirrel, this time a flying squirrel, which, although rare in Upstate New York, had been caught in a trap by W. K. Ayer in his home on the west side of Cazenovia Lake.

Camilla (Davis) Viall remembers Fitch and his squirrels. "He did have squirrels trained. They'd sit in the palm of his hand and kind of rub their eyes like they were just waking up, then he'd give them a nut," she remembered. Theckla Constable Ledyard also remembers that. "As young kids, you counted it a real treat to run into Jim and his pet red squirrel on Albany Street," she said. "He kept the squirrel in his shirt pocket and it would pop out looking for a handout of grapes that Jim kept for him."

In 1950, Lula L. Moon wrote a poem about "Old Jim" that was published in the *Cazenovia Republican*, in which she recalled:

If one should meet
Him on the street, he'd reach inside his coat
For the pet squirrel he had trained. 'Twould sit
Upon his arm, and turn somersault.
Then, from the bulging pocket of his worn,
Old, rust-brown coat, Old Jim would take out a nut.
"Here's your reward!" he'd say. "Hey! Not so fast!"
The squirrel, nut in mouth, had disappeared
Inside his coat. With wave of hand, Old Jim
Was on his way.

Amid the numerous traits and stories for which Jim Fitch was famous in and around Cazenovia, both during and after his life, one thing about him stands high above the rest—both literally and figuratively. During his years as a steeplejack, Fitch painted the steeple and the weathervane of the Cazenovia Presbyterian Church on Albany Street at least four times in as many decades. Apparently, nearly every time he was up there—163 feet above the ground—he would also perform various aerial and acrobatic stunts using the weathervane as his support.

The first record of it was in the October 6, 1921, issue of the *Cazenovia Republican*, which reported that Fitch performed "various acrobatic stunts" from atop the church steeple while he was working on it. His stunts included doing a headstand with arms outstretched, hanging by one hand and one foot, hanging by his hands only, lying on top of the weathervane itself (which is in the form of a fish) "and various other hair raising attitudes." Even more interesting, Fitch's friend Walter G. Chard took multiple pictures of the derring-do, both from the ground and from an upper window in the Ford house west of the church. The sepia photos were put on display in the window of C. H. Rouse's general store window for the community to see. "I remember well climbing onto the roof of a nearby house with my 4×5 Reflex Graflex to take the pictures of Jim," Chard told the *Cazenovia Republican* in 1950. "I took about a dozen pictures of Jim doing stunts on the steeple and gave him a set of 11x14 enlargements."

In June 1933, Fitch again painted the church steeple, and was again seen standing on his head "with his feet in the stratosphere putting his trust in a lightning rod and two strong arms," according to the *Cazenovia Republican*. "Jim always paints the steeple, and standing on his head is just part of the business." In 1941, the *Cazenovia Republican* published a feature story about Fitch, his circus career, and his life in Cazenovia after his retirement from the sawdust ring. According to the article—which printed on the front page one of Chard's photos of Fitch doing a "double hand horizontal" stunt on the steeple—the weathervane on the church was six feet, six inches long and weighed eighty pounds. "Jim used to lift it off its base, rest it on his shoulders while tying a rope to it, then lower it to the ground for another treatment of goldleaf." The *Cazenovia Republican* took pleasure in reporting one year later that its feature on Fitch won second place in the New York state weekly newspaper awards, best feature story category. The judges called the article "an excellent example of a local story marked by dash and vividness."

Fitch spent his final years in Cazenovia, continuing his work as a steeplejack and jack-of-all-trades as well as his reputation as a colorful local character. In the 1940s, Aikman wrote of his friend Fitch, "He is today as I know him—as I have always known him—hard as steel (he's just muscle and bone), erect, tattooed, grey haired, his nose pushed in by fistic encounters of by-gone days. Yet Jim's still tough, he is old in experience but he's still young in spirit. I can see him now—walking briskly down the street, more spry than any lad of sixteen, stopping to pet some dog (he loves animals), speaking cheerfully to all who greet him. . . . He's always clean-shaven, and spotlessly clean. Jim is never anything but a perfect gentleman with ladies."

In September 1947, it was reported that Fitch had temporarily lost the use of both his legs and was being cared for in the Smith nursing home in Unadilla Flats, near Leonardsville. In 1950, Fitch was becoming something of a local legend, and the *Cazenovia Republican* printed the six-stanza poem about Fitch by Lula L. Moon and reminiscences about Fitch by his friends and acquaintances. According to one report at this time, some of Fitch's friends took the former aerialist to the circus in his old age and his entrance into the big top was like royalty. "All the performers knew him and he knew all their grandparents."

Jim Fitch died on April 9, 1952, at age seventy-seven. Services were held by the Reverend F. N. Darling at the Smith Funeral Home, with burial in Evergreen Cemetery. According to the *Cazenovia Republican*, Fitch was survived by his two sisters, Mrs. Edward Marris of Cazenovia and Mrs. William Abrams of Baldwinsville. There was no formal obituary printed in the *Cazenovia Republican*; instead, the paper reprinted its award-winning 1941 feature article about Fitch, along with the photo of his acrobatics atop the Presbyterian church steeple. In the caption, *Cazenovia Republican* editor J. C. Peck wrote that he was publishing the photo again to keep a promise he had made to his friend three years prior that he would run the picture in connection with Fitch's death announcement "should the editor outlive his old time friend."

The Ox-Bow Incident

Great American Novel Written
by Cazenovia High School Teacher

Walter Van Tilburg Clark may not be a name that evokes immediate recognition for most people, but the title of Clark's first novel, *The Ox-Bow Incident*, is much more familiar. The book, published in 1940, was considered one of the top books of that year, was made into an Academy Award–nominated film starring Henry Fonda in 1943, was adapted to a stage production in 1976, and still is taught in high schools and colleges across the United States. While the novel is a Western, it is often considered to be the first modern Western in that it eschewed the typical clichés and formulaic plots of the genre and transcended into something more. Part of the book's mass appeal is that its themes are universal—it is a morality tale about justice, law, and mob violence that can fit into any genre; Clark just had a preference for the West.

And did you know that Clark lived in Cazenovia and taught English at Cazenovia High School when he wrote the book?

The Ox-Bow Incident is the story of two drifters who are drawn into a lynch mob to find and hang three men presumed to be cattle rustlers and the killers of a local man. When the mob comes across three riders and assumes their guilt in the face of unwavering pleas of innocence, the posse must decide what is the truth, how justice will be honestly served, and how they will live with themselves based on the decisions they make. As one description states, the book "examines law and order as well as culpability." Clark's biographer, Jackson J. Benson, more simply stated that the author and his book "turned the 'gallop and gun' popular Western on its head."

ENGLISH
MILTON KIRKPATRICK
WALTER E. MOON
WALTER V. T CLARK

31. School yearbook photograph of Walter Van Tilburg Clark, far right, author of the bestseller *The Ox-Bow Incident* and teacher at Cazenovia Central High School. Printed with permission given by Cazenovia Public Library.

Clark was in his early twenties when he began writing his Western novel during a cold, snowy winter in Cazenovia in 1937. Born in Maine, Clark had grown up in Reno, Nevada, where he went to college and lived until the early 1930s. His wife, Barbara, was from Elmira, New York, where the couple wed in 1933. In 1935, they moved to Cazenovia after Clark accepted a job teaching English at Cazenovia High School. The job had been offered to Clark by his brother-in-law Wayne Lowe, who had just become the district superintendent—a district that had only been created three years earlier by consolidating into one building students from the various single schoolhouses throughout the area.

The Clarks lived in Cazenovia for the next ten years, first in a house on Green Street and then, after returning in 1942 from a one-year sabbatical, in a house on Fenner Street. According to the 2004 book *The Ox-Bow Man: A Biography of Walter Van Tilburg Clark*, by Jackson J. Benson, Cazenovia had about eight hundred students in grades kindergarten through twelve in the 1930s. While there, Clark taught English and coached the basketball and tennis teams, and was faculty advisor to the drama club. According to Benson, Clark was well liked and respected by his students. Clark called teaching "an occupation I respect so much and am so fond of that it's kept me from doing anything like as much writing as I should have." Clark's most productive years in terms of both writing and publishing were during the 1930s and 1940s. "Thus, in Cazenovia from 1935 to 1945, he produced much of his writing while teaching high school, including two of his three published novels," according to the biographer.

Clark began writing *The Ox-Bow Incident* during Christmas vacation in 1937 and completed the first draft over Easter vacation 1938; he also completed another draft over Christmas vacation of 1938–39. Clark later told an interviewer he completed his first draft of the novel in one month, but revisions took two years. "It isn't the writing . . . it's the rewriting," he said. Clark later said his first draft of the book was an attempt to "do for the popular western with its myths and clichés what Cervantes did in burlesquing the chivalric romances of seventeenth century Spain in Don Quixote," according to Benson. He wanted to show the absurdity of the "two-gun cowboys stuffed with Sunday school virtues, and heroines who could go through a knock-down without getting a curl misplaced" and influence people to stop reading "such junk," he said. Clark said that in his revisions he decided to tackle the heavier issues of fascism and totalitarianism that he was seeing in Italy and Nazi Germany in the buildup to World War II, and relate it to the American West and how the Indians were treated by white men.

The book came out in 1940, published by Random House, and was a universal success both critically and commercially. The *New Yorker*'s Clifton Fadiman said *The Ox-Bow Incident* was his "unwavering choice for the year's finest first novel. It has many of the elements of an old-fashioned horse opera—monosyllabic cowpunchers, cattle rustlers, a Mae West lady, barroom brawls, shootings, lynchings, a villainous Mexican. But it bears about the same relation to an ordinary western as *The Maltese Falcon* does to a hack detective story. Not to put too fine a point on it, I think it's sort of what you might call a masterpiece." The *Cazenovia Republican* newspaper announced the publication of the book "by a member of the English faculty at the Cazenovia Central School," and quoted a review from the *New York Herald Tribune* calling the book "a new version of an old style of Western lynching bee. There is the required amount of excitement in this tale with a familiar theme but it stands by itself for its high grade of psychological and expert craftsmanship."

Three years after the publication of his first novel, Clark saw his creation come to the silver screen in a Hollywood version of *The Ox-Bow Incident* starring Henry Fonda, Mary Beth Hughes, and Dana Andrews. On October 15, 1943, the picture premiered at the Town Hall Theatre in Cazenovia, where it was so packed with people that "Mr. and Mrs. Clark, arriving a little late on Friday night, were unable to get seats and left the theatre without seeing the picture," according to reporting in the *Cazenovia Republican*. The movie was ultimately nominated for an Academy Award for best picture.

After the publication of *The Ox-Bow Incident*, Clark became famous and his writing came to be in high demand in major magazine publications, but he continued to teach in Cazenovia—working by day and writing late into the night. His second novel, *The City of Trembling Leaves* (1945), a semiautobiographical account of a sensitive boy growing up in Reno, Nevada, also was written in Cazenovia; while his third novel, *The Track of the Cat* (1949), about a Nevada cattle ranch threatened by a mountain lion, was written elsewhere. Both of those books were also made into movies, but neither the books nor their film counterparts achieved any sort of success comparable to *The Ox-Bow Incident*.

Clark also wrote short stories and poetry as well as novels; his short fiction earned him five O. Henry Prizes from 1941 to 1945, also while he lived and worked in Cazenovia. In 1950, he published his final book, a collection of short stories titled *The Watchful Gods*. Until his death in 1971, according to the Nevada Writers Hall of Fame, Clark "wrote furiously but published little." After moving away from Cazenovia in 1945, Clark taught English at the University of Montana in Missoula, at San Francisco State College, and at the University of Nevada at Reno, where he served as writer in residence from 1962 until his death in 1971 of cancer.

Bibliography

Books

Annual Report of the Adjutant General of the State of New York for the Year 1895. Albany, NY: Wynkoop Hallenbeck Crawford Co., 1896.

Atwell, Christine O. *Cazenovia Past and Present (Madison County, New York): A Descriptive and Historical Record of the Village*. Orlando: Florida Press, 1928.

The Balance, and Columbian Repository, vol. 1, for 1802. New York: Ezra Sampson, George Chittenden, and Harry Croswell, 1803.

Benson, Jackson J. *The Ox-Bow Man: A Biography of Walter Van Tilburg Clark*. Reno: Univ. of Nevada Press, 2004.

Blakeslee, Francis Durbin. *Personal Recollections and Impressions of Abraham Lincoln*. Gardena, CA: Spanish American Institute Press, 1927.

————. *How My Father Secured Lincoln's Autograph*. Privately printed. Spanish American Institute Press, 1927.

Bloomer, D. C. *Life and Writings of Amelia Bloomer*. Boston: Arena Publishing Co., 1895.

Bonney, Mrs. Catharina V. R. *A Legacy of Historical Gleanings*, 2 vols. Albany, NY: J. Munsell, 1875.

Brier, Bob. *Egyptomania: Our Three Thousand Year Obsession with the Land of the Pharaohs*. New York: Palgrave Macmillan, 2013.

Catalogue of the American Library of the Late Mr. George Brinley, of Hartford, Conn. Part 1. Hartford, CT: Press of the Case Lockwood and Brainhard Company, 1878.

Card, Lucia Zora. *Sawdust and Solitude*. Boston: Little, Brown, and Company, 1928.

Clark, Walter Van Tilburg. *The Ox-Bow Incident*. New York: Random House, 1940.

Connecticut Historical Society. *Lists and Returns of Connecticut Men in the Revolution, 1775–1783*. Hartford: Connecticut Historical Society, 1909.

Dandridge, Anne Spottswood, comp. *The Forman Genealogy*. Cleveland: The Forman-Bassett-Hatch Co., 1903.

Dyer, Frederick H. *A Compendium of the War of the Rebellion*. Des Moines: Dyer Publishing Company, 1908.

Ellsworth, Anzolette D. *New Woodstock and Vicinity Past and Present*. Cazenovia, NY: J. Loyster, 1901.

First Fifty Years of Cazenovia Seminary, 1825–1875. Cazenovia, NY: Nelson and Phillips, 1877.

Forman, Charles. *Three Revolutionary Soldiers: David Forman, Jonathan Forman, Thomas Marsh Forman*. Cleveland: The Forman-Bassett-Hatch Co., 1902.

Forman, Samuel S. *Annals of Cazenovia: 1793–1837*. Cazenovia, NY: Gleaner Press, 1982.

Fox, Charles Barnard. *Record of the Service of the Fifty-Fifth Regiment of Massachusetts Volunteer Infantry*. Cambridge, MA: The Press of John Wilson and Son, 1868.

Gillett, Fidelia Woolley. *Memoir of Rev. Edward Mott Woolley*. Boston: Abel Tompkins, 1855.

Gordon, Thomas F. *Gazetteer of the State of New York*. Philadelphia: T. K. and P. G. Collins, printers, 1836.

Greene, John Robert. *Generations of Excellence: An Illustrated History of Cazenovia Seminary*. Syracuse, NY: Syracuse Litho, 2000.

Greenwood, Grace. *Greenwood Leaves: A Collection of Sketches and Letters*. Boston: Ticknor, Reed, and Fields, 1850.

Grills, Russell. *Cazenovia: The Story of an Upland Community*. Cazenovia, NY: Cazenovia Preservation Foundation, 1977.

———. *Upland Idyll: Images of Cazenovia, New York, 1860–1900*. The State of New York Office of Parks, Recreation and Historic Preservation, 1993.

Grubbs, Frank E., Leslie E. Simon, and Serge J. Zaroodny. *Robert Harrington Kent 1886–1961, A Biographical Memoir*. Washington, DC: National Academy of Sciences, 1971.

Halstead, Murat. *The Life of Theodore Roosevelt*. Akron, OH: Saalfield Publishing, 1902.

Hammond, Luna M. *History of Madison County*. Syracuse, NY: Truair, Smith & Co., 1872.

Hanchett, William. *The Lincoln Murder Conspiracies*. Urbana: Univ. of Illinois Press, 1983.

Harvard College Class of 1910. *Harvard College Class of 1910, Fourth Report 1921*. Cambridge, MA: Crimson Printing Company, 1921.

Hawkswell, John. *Autobiography and Miscellaneous Writings of Elder W. W. Crane.* Syracuse, NY: A. W. Hall, 1891.

Johnston, Henry P., ed. *Record of Connecticut Men in Military and Naval Service During the War of the Revolution, 1775–1783.* Hartford, CT: Case, Lockwood & Brainard Co., 1889.

Leavengood, Betty. *Tucson Hiking Guide.* Boulder, CO: Pruett Publishing Company, 1991.

Lists and Returns of Connecticut Men in the Revolution, 1775–1783. Collections of the Connecticut Historical Society, vol. 12. Hartford: Connecticut Historical Society, 1909.

Matson, William N. *Reports of Cases, Argued and Determined in The Supreme Court of Errors of the State of Connecticut.* Second edition. New York: Banks & Brothers, Law Publishers and Booksellers, 1873.

Military Minutes of the Council of Appointment of the State of New York, 1783–1821, vol. 1. Albany, NY: James B. Lyon, 1901.

Murphy, Eloise Cronin. *Theodore Roosevelt's Night Ride to the Presidency.* Blue Mountain Lake, NY: Adirondack Museum, 1977.

Phisterer, Frederick, comp. *New York in the War of the Rebellion, 1861–1865.* Albany, NY: J. B. Lyon Company, 1912.

Pierce, John, United States War Department. *Pierce's Register: Register of Certificates Issued by John Pierce, Esq., "paymaster general and commissioner of army accounts for the US" to officers and soldiers of the Continental Army under act of July 4, 1783,* issue 2. Baltimore: Reprinted for Clearfield Company by Genealogical Publishing Company, 2012.

Rivette, Barbara S. *Grover Cleveland: Fayetteville's Hometown Boy.* Fayetteville, NY, 1987.

Severance, Henry. *Owahgena: Being a History of the Town and Village of Cazenovia.* Edited and annotated by Roberta L. Hendrix Severance. Cazenovia, NY: Cazenovia Public Library, 1984.

Shaw, Cass Ledyard. *The Ledyard Family in America.* West Kennebunk, ME: Phoenix Publishing, 1993.

Smith, Donald B. *Mississauga Portraits: Ojibwe Voices from Nineteenth-Century Canada.* Toronto: Univ. of Toronto Press, 2013.

Smith, James H. *History of Madison County.* Syracuse, NY: D. Mason, 1880.

Smith, John E., ed. *Our Country and its People: Descriptive and Biographical Record of Madison County, New York.* Boston: Boston History Co., 1899.

Soldiers and Sailors. *The Three Bummers, and Other Stories of the War.* New York: John W. Lovell Company, 1887.

State of New York. *Public Papers of Daniel D. Tompkins, Governor of New York, 1807– 1817, military,* Vol. 1. New York and Albany, NY: Wynkoop Hallenbeck Crawford Co., 1898.

Summerfield, John, alias Sahgahjewagahbahweh. *Sketch of Grammar of the Chippeway Language, to which is Added a Vocabulary of Some of the Most Common Words.* Cazenovia, NY: Press of J. F. Fairchild & Son. 1834.

SUNY ESF Faculty of Landscape Architecture. *Cultural Landscape Report Lorenzo State Historic Site, Cazenovia, New York.*

US Congress. *Biographical Directory of the United States Congress, 1774–1989.* Washington, DC: United States Congress, 1989.

White, David O. *Connecticut's Black Soldiers, 1775–1783.* Chester, CT: Pequot Press, 1973.

Wilson, Jean Ellen. *Legendary Locals of Fort Pierce.* Charleston, SC: Arcadia Publishing, 2014.

Wilson, Rufus Rockwell. *Intimate Memories of Lincoln.* Elmira, NY: The Primavera Press, 1945.

Articles

"60 Years Old, Stands on Head on Church Steeple." *Cazenovia Republican,* June 15, 1933, 1.

"91 Years Old Today." *Cazenovia Republican,* June 26, 1941, 2.

"105 From Town of Cazenovia." *Cazenovia Republican,* May 16, 1918, 1.

Abell, Jabez W. "1816, 'The Year Without a Summer.'" *Cazenovia Republican,* March 9, 1939, 1.

"Action of the Trustees Concerning Dr. Blakeslee's Resignation." *Cazenovia Republican,* July 2, 1908, 4.

"After Denying Rumors." *Cazenovia Republican,* February 7, 1895, 4.

Aikman, William O. "Everybody Knows Jim." *The Mirror* 84, no. 2 (Winter 1942): 17, 26–28.

Aldous, Joan F. "Theodore Roosevelt's Midnight Ride." *The Post Star* [Glens Falls, NY], November 24, 2008.

"Andersonville Prison." American Battlefield Trust website, www.battlefields .org.

"Annie Robbins, wife." *Cazenovia Republican,* May 5, 1892, 3.

"Anniversary Exercises." *Cazenovia Republican*, June 22, 1905, 1.

Anonymous. "Cazenovia Seminary and 100 Canadian Youths." *Hay Bay Guardian* 18 (2010): 4–5.

"At His Boyhood's Home." *New York Times*, July 20, 1887.

Ayres, Edward. "African Americans and the American Revolution." historyisfun .org (Jamestown Settlement and American Revolution Museum at Yorktown), accessed 2/4/2019.

"Back in Fayetteville." *Syracuse Standard*, July 20, 1887, 4.

"Bergman, June. "Sad Story of 'Crazy Luce' May Be a Legend or a Fact." *Cazenovia Republican*, June 9, 1971, 3.

"Biographical Sketch." *The Balance, and Columbian Repository*, April 20, 1802, 125.

Blake, Henry W. "Cazenovia Reflections." *Kindergarten News*, 7, no. 2 (October 1896): 66–67

"Blakeslee Brings Autographs of Lincoln and Webster Here." *Poughkeepsie Eagle-News*, August 18, 1934, 1.

Blakeslee, F. D. "Lincoln As I Knew Him." *Cazenovia Republican*, April 23, 1936, 10.

Blakeslee, Francis D. "Sidelights on Abraham Lincoln." *Cazenovia Republican*, February 9, 1939, 9.

Bloomer Costume—Attention to All." *Madison County Whig*, July 16, 1851, 1.

"The Bloomer Costume." *Madison County Journal*, August 21, 1851, 2.

"Bloomerism—A Latter Day Fragment." *Cazenovia Gazette*, December 31, 1851, 4.

"Burned to Death." *East Oregonian* [Pendleton, OR], March 2, 1908, 7.

Cadwell, A. S. "Brief Biography of Samuel S. Forman." *Albany Atlas and Argus*, March 16, 1861.

"Cazenovia Boy In France Given Croix de Guerre." *Cazenovia Republican*, January 9, 1919, 1.

"Cazenovia Honored." *Cazenovia Republican*, July 21, 1887, 2.

"Cazenovia's Oldest Resident, Mrs. Sarah Robbins, 105, Dies." *Cazenovia Republican*, December 16, 1948, 1.

"Cazenovia Woman Has Four Sons in Service." *Cazenovia Republican*, June 20, 1918, 1.

"Cecil Donovan Exhibits Art." *Cazenovia Republican*, June 12, 1924, 1.

"Cecil Donovan Exhibits Art." *Cazenovia Republican*, July 31, 1930, 4.

"Cecil Donovan In Midst of Big Drive." *Cazenovia Republican*, May 9, 1918, 1.

"Cecil Donovan off for France." *Cazenovia Republican*, August 9, 1917, 1.

"Cecil Donovan Writes of His Work in France." *Cazenovia Republican*, September 27, 1917, 1.

"Cecil V. Donovan has been cited for a French War Cross." *Cazenovia Republican*, June 13, 1918, 1.

"Chester C. Kent Named Trust Officer." *Cazenovia Republican*, January 12, 1922, 1.

"Chester Kent Dies Former Resident." *Cazenovia Republican*, April 6, 1950, 1.

"Cleveland at Clinton." *Cazenovia Republican*, July 14, 1887, 2.

"Cleveland Tree Alive at Lorenzo." *Cazenovia Republican*, October 11, 1972, 4.

"The Cold Weather for a Week Past." *Ontario Repository* (Canandaigua, NY) June 11, 1816, 3.

"Comrade Stevenson of the G.A.R." *Cazenovia Republican*, April 17, 1884, 3.

"Copy of a letter from Col. John Lincklaen." *New-York Evening Post*, February 27, 1802, 2.

"Coroner's Jury Holds Inquest Over Body." *Los Angeles Herald*, February 22, 1908, 7.

"County and State News Paragraphs." *Brookfield Courier*, March 16, 1921, 1.

"Crazy Luce." *Cortland Republican*, March 15, 1836, 1.

"Crazy Luce Wandered Hereabouts 140 Years Ago Jilted by Her Lover." *Cazenovia Republican*, August 10, 1939, 1.

"Death Former Resident." *Cazenovia Republican*, May 20, 1943, 1.

"Death of Dr. E. M. Kent." *Cazenovia Republican*, September 13, 1917, 5.

"Death of Former Resident." *Cazenovia Republican*, January 22, 1948, 1.

"Death of Mr. S. W. Kent." *Cazenovia Republican*, January 30, 1913, 1.

"Descendant of Slaves 102 Monday." *Cazenovia Republican*, March 8, 1945, 1.

"Died—On the 19th inst." *The Pilot*, December 21, 1820, 2.

"Dies at 91." *Cazenovia Republican*, December 11, 1941, 2.

"Discovery of Another Canoe in Lake Owahgena." *Cazenovia Republican*, October 25, 1865, 2.

"Dr. Blakeslee, Former Seminary Head, Recalls Clerks Helping Defend City of Washington Against Confederates." *Cazenovia Republican*, May 27, 1937, 9.

"Dr. Blakeslee is Ninety-Six." *Potsdam Herald-Recorder*, Feb. 27, 1942, 4.

"Dr. F. D. Blakeslee, Authority on Abraham Lincoln, Dies." *Los Angeles Times*, Sept. 13, 1942.

"Dr. Francis D. Blakeslee, Oldest Syracuse Alumnus, Dies in West, Aged 96." *Syracuse Herald-Journal*, September 15, 1942, 12.

"Dr. Robert H. Kent, Hall of Fame Inductee." United States Army Ordinance Corps website, www.goordnance.army.mil/hof/1969/kent.html.

"The Early History of Madison County." *Cazenovia Republican*, April 20, 1876, 1.

"The Eastern State Journal." *The Golden Rule, and Odd-Fellows Companion*, May 1, 1847, 302.

"Echoes of the Outing." *New York Times,* July 21, 1887.

"Ed. Farley Recalls Boyhood." *Cazenovia Republican,* January 27, 1944, 1.

"Elizabeth Smith Miller Cazenovia Home." Freethought Trail website, accessed March 2019, https://freethought-trail.org/trail-map/location:elizabeth-smith-miller-cazenovia-home/.

"Elizabeth Smith Miller Feminist, Philanthropist and Social Reformer." Retrieved from http://www.womenhistoryblog.com/2012/10/elizabeth-smith-miller.html.

Enns, Gregory. "Final resting spot of 'bravest woman' an unmarked grave?" *Indian River Magazine.* Retrieved from indianrivermag.com.

———. "Unmarked grave of 'bravest woman' circus performer." *Indian River Magazine.* Posted in April 2017. Retrieved from indianrivermag.com.

"Ensign Stanley Commands Submarine Chaser." *Cazenovia Republican,* June 13, 1918, 1.

"Ensign Stanley Kent In Naval Battle." *Cazenovia Republican,* November 28, 1918, 1.

"Errata." *Cazenovia Republican,* November 1, 1865, 2.

"Escaped from Rebel Prison." *Cazenovia Republican,* March 15, 1865, 4.

"Ex-Cazenovia Seminary Head Still Excels as Wood Cutter." *Cazenovia Republican,* April 6, 1939, 1.

"The Experience of William Madge in Dixie." *Cazenovia Republican,* April 12, 1865, 4.

Fadiman, Clifton. "Make Way for Mr. Clark." *The New Yorker,* October 12, 1940.

"'Fair View' Pineapple Farm." *Cazenovia Republican,* November 16, 1905, 1.

"Firemen's Convention." *Cazenovia Republican,* June 26, 1890, 3.

"Fire of the Flint." *The Balance, and Columbian Repository,* March 9, 1802, 78.

"The Following Letter Has Been Received." *Cazenovia Republican,* September 19, 1918, 7.

"The Following Letters Have Been Received." *Cazenovia Republican,* February 21, 1918, 1.

"Footnote to History." *Cazenovia Republican,* October 11, 1978, 6.

"Former Cazenovian and Two Sons in Who's Who." *Cazenovia Republican,* November 29, 1923, 1.

"Friends of Miss Susan Blow." *Cazenovia Republican,* March 30, 1916, 5.

"From the Albany *Argus,* July, Celebration of the Abolition of Slavery." *Madison Observer,* July 11, 1827, 2.

"From the *Boston Gazette,* August 19." *New-York Evening Post,* August 21, 1816, 2.

"From the *Whitestown Gazette.*" *Otsego Herald: Or, Western Advertiser,* April 22, 1801, 1.

"Glimpse of the Grand Review." *Potsdam Herald-Recorder*, November 8, 1929, 7.

"A Grand Old Man—Col. Charles D. Miller, the famous abolitionist talks entertainingly of life." *Syracuse Evening Herald*, June 15, 1893.

"A Great Demonstration." *Fayetteville Weekly Recorder*, July 21, 1887, 6.

Grigas, C. "Zora! The Bravest Woman in The World." *Indian River Magazine* (December 2010): 13–17, 21–22.

Greenwood, Grace. "A Night of Years." *The Golden Rule, and Odd-Fellows Companion*, April 3, 1847, 225–27.

"Hayes & Wheeler Club." *Cazenovia Republican*, July 13, 1876, 3.

"He Can Recall Lincoln Death." *Los Angeles Times*, February 12, 1929, 1.

"Hello, Central? Gimme the Market." *Cazenovia Republican*, May 23, 1973, 4.

"Hilliard-Card." *Cazenovia Republican*, February 8, 1900, 1.

"Historical Reminiscences." *Cazenovia Standard*, January 22, 1879, 2.

"Historic Buildings of Urbana." Retrieved from https://historic-urbana-webmap .netlify.com.

"Indian Legend Depicted in Colorful Ceremony." *Cazenovia Republican*, October 13, 1938, 1.

"Indian Log Canoe Part of Caz Lore." *Cazenovia Republican*, June 27, 1979, 5.

"In the May Issue of the *Ladies Home Journal*." *Cazenovia Republican*, May 8, 1924, 2.

"Jim Fitch, Old Circus Man, Dies." *Cazenovia Republican*, April 10, 1952, 1.

"Jim Fitch Paints Steeple." *Cazenovia Republican*, August 18, 1921, 1.

"Jim Fitch Taming Flying Squirrel." *Cazenovia Republican*, January 24, 1924, 1.

"John Stevenson Buried." *Cazenovia Republican*, June 2, 1881, 3.

"John Stevenson Rejoicing." *Cazenovia Republican*, December 1, 1898, 3.

Jones, Todd. "29th Regiment Connecticut Volunteers Fought More Than One War." Posted on November 23, 2016. Retrieved from https://connecticuthistory.org /the-29th-regiment-connecticut-volunteers-fought-more-than-one-war.

"Journal by Major William Gould, of the New Jersey Infantry, During an Expedition into Pennsylvania in 1794." *Proceedings of the New Jersey Historical Society* 3 (1848–49): 173–91.

"Jubilee of the Methodist Episcopal Zion's Church." *Syracuse Daily Journal*, October 30, 1879.

"The July Issue of 'The Ladies Home Journal'." *Cazenovia Republican*, July 22, 1926, 5.

"Jury Lists—A Colored Man Drawn as a Grand Juror." *Syracuse Daily Courier*, September 17, 1880

Kent, Olney Brown. "Nunc Dimittis." *Poultry Science*, 35, no. 6 (November 1, 1956), 1400.

"The Kindergarten." *Cazenovia Republican*, February 26, 1891, 3.

"Kindergarten Conference." *Cazenovia Republican*, August 6, 1896, 3.

"The Kindergarten Convention." *Cazenovia Republican*, August 27, 1896, 3.

"Kindergarten Nursery." *Cazenovia Republican*, January 8, 1891, 3.

"Late last Friday afternoon." *Cazenovia Republican*, November 21, 1889, 1.

"Legend of Owahgena Lake." *Cazenovia Republican*, August 10, 1916, 1.

"A Letter from Erieville." *Chenango American*, February 26, 1885, 2.

"Letters from Cazenovia Folks 'Over There.'" *Cazenovia Republican*, November 14, 1918, 1.

"Letters to the Editor—Club House, study hall and lunch room." *Cazenovia Republican*, August 25, 1976, 4.

"Life in the Shadows: The First Generation John and Helen Lincklaen's Residency: 1808–1843," wall display text, Lorenzo State Historic Site, Cazenovia, NY.

"List of Letters." *The Pilot*, January 5, 1820, 3.

"Looks to Centennial of Lafayette visit." *Utica Daily Press*, May 30, 1925.

"Madame Zora." *Cazenovia Republican*, May 18, 1899, 1.

"Many Cazenovia Pupils Pass Regents." *Cazenovia Republican*, July 3, 1913, 4.

"Many Curios at Cazenovia's Public Library." *Cazenovia Republican*, May 30, 1912, 1.

"Married." *Madison County Eagle*, October 25, 1843, 3.

"Miss Blow's Lecture." *Cazenovia Republican*, August 21, 1902, 1.

"Missouri Women in History: Susan E. Blow." *Missouri Historical Review* 61, no. 2 (January 1967): back cover.

"Miss Susan E. Blow." *Cazenovia Republican*, August 16, 1900, 3.

"More Letters from Cazenovia Soldiers." *Cazenovia Republican*, November 29, 1917, 1.

"More Local History Given." *Cazenovia Republican*, June 26, 1958, 7.

"Mr. Cecil Donovan has returned." *Cazenovia Republican*, June 8, 1916, 2.

"Mr. Cecil Donovan, Son of Mr. and Mrs. W. T. Donovan." *Cazenovia Republican*, June 7, 1917, 1.

"Mr. Chester C. Kent, Esq." *Cazenovia Republican*, May 11, 1905, 5.

"Mr. John Stevenson." *Cazenovia Republican*, October 15, 1914, 4.

"Mrs. Berlin G. Brann." *Cazenovia Republican*, September 20, 1917, 5.

"Mrs. John Stevenson died." *Cazenovia Republican*, October 20, 1887, 3.

"The Mummy at the Public Library." *Cazenovia Republican,* January 24, 1895, 3.

"Mummy is a 'He.'" *Cazenovia Republican,* April 12, 2006, 1.

"Mummy Makes Hospital Visit." *Cazenovia Republican,* December 13, 2017, 1.

"Mummy Notes: How an Egyptian Mummy Found its Way to Cazenovia in 1894." *Cazenovia Republican,* May 16, 2007, 12.

"Mummy Notes: Part II—How an Egyptian Mummy Found its Way to Cazenovia in 1894." *Cazenovia Republican,* May 23, 2007, 18–19.

"The Mummy Returns." *Cazenovia Republican,* March 15, 2006, 1.

"The Mummy Tea." *Cazenovia Republican,* February 7, 1895, 3.

"New Guinea." *Utica Sunday Tribune,* December 19, 1909, 1.

"A Night of Years." *Cazenovia Republican,* January 9, 1856, 1.

"A Night of Years." *Jeffersonian Democrat,* February 17, 1865, 1.

"Obituaries—Robert H. Kent." *Physics Today,* 14, no. 7 (1961): 68.

"Obituary, Alberta Leroy Robbins." *Cazenovia Republican,* January 31, 1907, 1.

"Obituary." *Cazenovia Republican,* October 13, 1869, 3.

"Odd Characters Who Trod Roads Fifty Years Ago." *Cazenovia Republican,* July 16, 1931, 8.

"Old Indian Birch Canoe Sunk in Cazenovia 72 Years Ago." *Cazenovia Republican,* September 21, 1933.

"Old Indian Canoe Raised from Lake." *Cazenovia Republican,* February 13, 1913, 1.

"Old Jim." *Cazenovia Republican,* June 22, 1950, 1.

"Old Soldier Loses Life." *Los Angeles Herald,* February 21, 1908, 7.

"Old Time Circus Man Livened up Cazenovia." *Cazenovia Republican,* July 6, 1977, 4.

"One of Jim Fitch's Admirers Reminisces." *Cazenovia Republican,* August 10, 1950, 1.

"The Origin of Bloomers." *Cazenovia Republican,* July 5, 1865, 2.

"Out of the Wilderness." *New York Times,* July 19, 1887.

"Ox Bow Author Dies in Nevada." *Cazenovia Republican,* November 17, 1971.

"Pathetic Story of 'Crazy Luce' Printed in Cortland for Pedlars." *Cortland Democrat,* April 24, 1936, 1.

Peck, J. C. "The Cold Year of 1816 Contrasted with the Present Winter." *Cazenovia Republican* February 17, 1916, 1.

"Personal and Social Items." *Cazenovia Republican,* April 3, 1919, 5.

"Personal and Social Items." *Cazenovia Republican,* March 10, 1921, 5.

"Personal and Social Items." *Cazenovia Republican,* October 6, 1921, 5.

"Personal and Social Items." *Cazenovia Republican,* January 11, 1923, 2.

"Photograph, Clipping Increase Canoe Lore." *Cazenovia Republican,* October 1, 1969, 3.

"Plymouth Freeman—The Revolutionary War Cook to George Washington." *Hills and Hollows, newsletter of the Erieville-Nelson Heritage Society*, 2, no. 2 (May 2018): 1.

"The President at Manlius." *New York Times*, July 23, 1887.

"President Cleveland and Bride Guests at Cazenovia 50 Years Ago—Feted and Dined." *Cazenovia Republican*, July 22, 1937, 1.

"The President in Cazenovia." *Cazenovia Republican*, July 14, 1887, 3.

"The President's Escape." *Syracuse Sunday Herald*, July 17, 1887.

"The President's Visit to Central New York." *Fayetteville Weekly Recorder*, July 21, 1887, 2.

"A Prominent Man Gone—Robert J. Hubbard is Mourned in the Village." *Cazenovia Republican*, December 22, 1904, 1.

"Private W. H. B. Kent in France." *Cazenovia Republican*, September 12, 1918, 1.

"Prof. and Mrs. Cecil Donovan and daughter." *Cazenovia Republican*, June 11, 1925, 5.

"Prof. and Mrs. Cecil Donovan." *Cazenovia Republican*, May 29, 1924, 5.

"Prof. Cecil Donovan of this place." *Cazenovia Republican*, September 1, 1927, 9.

"Quotes and Comments." *Cazenovia Republican*, June 29, 1977, 4.

"Quotes and Comments." *Cazenovia Republican*, July 13, 1977, 4.

"Quotes and Comments." *Cazenovia Republican*, July 20, 1977, 4.

"Read Republican for Fifty-Three Years." *Cazenovia Republican*, June 8, 1911, 1.

"Robert H. Kent." *Cazenovia Republican*, February 16, 1961, 3.

"Robert Kent, Expert Ballistician, Promoted to Captain." *Cazenovia Republican*, April 17, 1919, 1.

"Roosevelt Day—The Governor at Cazenovia." *Cazenovia Republican*, October 25, 1900, 1.

"Seminary Items." *Cazenovia Republican*, May 28, 1903, 4.

Seventy Six. "Revolutionary Reminiscences—No. 2." *Evening Post* [New York], Jan. 14, 1852, 1.

"Sewer Connections." *Cazenovia Republican*, July 4, 1895, 3.

"Shoots Her Persecutor." *Cazenovia Republican*, October 25, 1900, 1.

"Shot by an Actress." *Florida Star*, October 26, 1900, 4.

"Social and Personal Items." *Cazenovia Republican*, June 8, 1933, 5.

"Soldiers Write Home of Experiences in Camp." *Cazenovia Republican*, December 6, 1917, 4.

"Soldiers Write of Camp Life to Parents in Cazenovia." *Cazenovia Republican*, November 1, 1917, 1.

"Story of 'Crazy Lucy' Written for Republican." *Cazenovia Republican*, July 8, 1915, 1.

"A Story of Love and Healing: Native American Tribes Bond Over Cazenovia Wedding." *Cazenovia Republican*, June 10, 2015, 1.

Stothers, Richard B. "The Great Tambora Eruption in 1815 and Its Aftermath." *Science* 224, no. 4654 (June 15, 1984): 1191–98.

"Suicide of Mr. John Madge." *Cazenovia Republican*, October 24, 1866, 2.

"Sunken Canoe a Vestige of Love." *Cazenovia Republican*, April 5, 1967, 8.

"Sunken Canoe Photographed." *Cazenovia Republican*, September 17, 1969, 1.

"Susan E. Blow." *St. Louis Post-Dispatch*. March 28, 1916, 3.

"Talked to Lincoln Later than Cabinet officers." *Cazenovia Republican*, April 22, 1909, 1.

Taylor, M. A. Letter to the editor. *Jeffersonian Democrat*, February 17, 1865, 1.

"To Have a Mummy." *Cazenovia Republican*, April 5, 1894, 3.

"To Interest the Boys." *Cazenovia Republican*, October 17, 1901, 1.

"The Village Election." *Cazenovia Republican*, March 22, 1900, 1.

Walter, George W. "Chips and Savings—Crazy Luce." *Mid-York Weekly* [Hamilton, NY], June 19, 1947, 8.

"Walter Clark Couldn't Get In to See Own Movie." *Cazenovia Republican*, October 21, 1943, 1.

Werme, Eric. "1816: The Year Without a Summer, A New Hampshire Perspective." June 7, 2016, Wermenh.com.

"Western Novel by Cazenovian among New Books." *Cazenovia Republican*, October 10, 1940.

"Winter in June!" *Geneva Gazette*, June 12, 1816, 3.

"With Buffalo Bill's Wild West Show 2½ Years." *Cazenovia Republican*, August 7, 1941, 1; reprinted April 17, 1952, 6.

"Wm. T. Donovan Dies." *Cazenovia Republican*, July 2, 1936, 1.

"A Woman's Rights Woman." *Cazenovia Republican*, April 25, 1872, 1.

Wood, Gillen D'Arcy. "1816, The Year without a Summer." *BRANCH: Britain, Representation and Nineteenth-Century History*. Edited by Dino Franco Felluga. Extension of *Romanticism and Victorianism on the Net*. (December 2011), accessed online 2018.

Yared, Ephram. "55th Massachusetts Infantry Regiment (1863–1865)." Posted March 15, 2016. www.blackpast.org/african-american-history/55th-massachusetts-infantry-regiment-1863-1865/.

"Zora Card." *Cazenovia Republican*, December 3, 1936, 6.

"Zora Card Dies." *Cazenovia Republican*, November 12, 1936, 1.

"Zora Card's Book in Library." *Cazenovia Republican*, April 26, 1928, 1.

"Zora Card Shot Joe Pazen." *St. Louis Republic*, October 18, 1900, 7.

Television Programs

History Detectives, season 5, episode 3, "GAR Photograph," directed by C. Tine, aired on July 9, 2007, on PBS.

Archives

Abraham Lincoln Presidential Library and Museum, Springfield, IL

Cazenovia historical archives, Cazenovia Public Library, Cazenovia, NY

Cazenovia town records, Cazenovia, NY

Cazenovia village records, Cazenovia, NY

Evergreen Cemetery records, Cazenovia, NY

Frederic and Jean Williams Archives, Cazenovia College, Cazenovia, NY

Jonathan Forman Papers, archives and special collections, University of Pittsburgh, Pittsburgh, PA

Lincoln Financial Foundation Collection, Allen County Public Library, Fort Wayne, IN

Lorenzo State Historic Site archives, NYS Office of Parks, Recreation & Historic Preservation, Cazenovia, NY

    Bills of sale

    Biographical list

    John Lincklaen Correspondence

    Ledyard Family Papers

    Manumission records

    Mary Fitzhugh Ledyard diary

    Samuel Forman store ledgers and day books, 1802–7

    Samuel Forman papers

Madison County, NY, records and archives

New York State Archives, Albany, NY

New York State Military Museum and Veterans Research Center, NYS Division of Military and Naval Affairs (https://dmna.ny.gov)

US National Archives, Washington, DC
    Army land warrants
    Civil War muster rolls
    Civil War pension records
    New York State census records
    Revolutionary War records
    US Federal Census records

Newspapers

Binghamton Press
Brookfield Courier
Cazenovia Pilot
Cazenovia Republican
Cazenovia Standard
Chenango American
Cortland Republican
Cortland Democrat
Eastern State Journal
East Oregonian
Florida Star
Geneva Gazette
Golden Rule and Odd-Fellows Companion
Hancock Jeffersonian
Jeffersonian Democrat
Los Angeles Herald

Los Angeles Times
Madison Observer
Mid-York Weekly
New York Evening Post
New York Times
Ontario Repository [Canandaigua, NY]
Otsego Herald, of Western Advertiser
Potsdam Herald-Recorder
Poughkeepsie Eagle-News
St. Louis Post-Dispatch
St. Louis Republic
Syracuse Herald Journal
Syracuse Journal
Syracuse Standard
Weekly Recorder [Fayetteville, NY]

Websites

Ancestry Library.com
Cazenovia Public Library Digital Archives, http://cazenovia.advantage-preservation.com
Smithsonian Institution, www.si.edu
US Army Ordinance Corps, www.goordnance.army.mil
US House of Representatives, Congressional profiles, http://history.house.gov/Congressional-Overview/Profiles

Interviews/Correspondence

Lynda Copper
Michael Burlingame
Russell Grills

ERICA BARNES is a teacher and historian. She compiled the "Years Ago in History" section of the *Cazenovia Republican* newspaper for five years. This job entailed countless hours perusing historic issues of the *Republican* and its predecessor papers, finding interesting news items from years ago that dovetailed with current events and concerns, and compiling them into a file each week of the year. In 2017, she assisted the public library in creating and implementing a multifaceted celebration of the village's history for the 225th anniversary of Cazenovia's founding.

JASON EMERSON is an independent historian and journalist. He is the author or editor of seven books about Abraham Lincoln and his family, and the former editor of the *Cazenovia Republican* newspaper. Jason has also published dozens of history articles in both popular magazines and academic journals, and he has been a history expert on multiple television shows, including on the History Channel, H2, Book TV, American History TV, and CNBC. His website is www.jasonemerson.com.